Matched In Heaven

By
Angela Page

D1522926

Eternal Press
A division of Damnation Books, LLC.
P.O. Box 3931
Santa Rosa, CA 95402-9998
www.eternalpress.biz

Matched In Heaven
by Angela Page

Digital ISBN: 978-1-62929-328-8
Print ISBN: 978-1-62929-329-5

Cover art by: Dawné Dominique
Edited by: Kim Richards

Copyright 2015 Angela Page

Printed in the United States of America
Worldwide Electronic & Digital Rights
Worldwide English Language Print Rights

This book is a work of fiction. Characters,
names, places and incidents either are the
product of the author's imagination or are used
fictitiously, and any resemblance to any actual
persons, living or dead, events, or locales is
entirely coincidental.

For K, J and M—RIP

Prologue

Bad Priest

When the young and handsome Jesuit priest, Padre Mateo, ascended to the spirit world, he heard the sound of "tsk-tsk." As he passed through the white light, he continued hearing the sound of disapproval. Then it suddenly stopped and a voice announced, "Bad priest."

Padre Mateo had sired several children with the parish maid in a Peruvian village. He fleeced the natives of their worldly goods for payment for services. At age thirty-five, he contracted deadly typhoid fever giving last rites to a dying Indian.

The now dead priest thought he escaped judgment until a voice remarked, "Dude, what were you thinking?" Then he knew he was screwed.

Padre Mateo was sent to a group of corrupt, perverted, and nasty clergymen and women for intense rehabilitation. It's one thing to behave badly on Earth, but to do it while representing religion was another issue. The members of the Heavenly Council were especially angry about the bad PR. They were always doing damage control by sending kind and thoughtful clergy back to Earth to improve religion's reputation. The last thing the council needed was everyone on Earth losing faith.

While in spiritual rehab, Father Mateo had an epiphany. He pitched the Heavenly Council the idea of a support group and matchmaking service for guilty priests who left behind young children and destitute women. Long before the Earth developed personal ads, Internet, and speed dating, Father Mateo set up a dedicated celestial matchmaking service. He convinced the council to give him the power to help clergymen match the partners they left behind on Earth and provide for their bastard children. The group was named Guilty Priests/ Young Families, GPYF. He was so successful that the council eventually gave him non-clergy departed souls to help. "Guilty priests" became "guilty partners" with Father Mateo—now rebranded Marcel—as the group leader.

Marcel resembled a middle-aged beatnik poet with a beret, a goatee, and a diamond earring in his left ear. He stood at five-nine, had close-cropped salt-and-pepper hair, and walked with a relaxed swagger in his usual jeans, loose silk monogrammed shirts, and cowboy boots. He recruited, facilitated, and coached guilty departed spouses. He was also in charge of earthly matchmaking. The spirit guides were pleased with Marcel's progress and impressed by how many people he helped.

As the dead spouses arrived, riddled with guilt, he guided them with his pastoral charms. He counseled them on how best to climb the spiritual ladder by taking care of unfinished business on Earth from Heaven. He was responsible for matching thousands of widows and widowers on Earth with new partners.

Marcel reached an impasse with two long-standing members. Mimi and Jake needed his intervention. Both left behind partners and young sons, along with other complications. They only had one thing in common: guilt. Otherwise they hated each other.

As they passed from Earth to the spirit world, Mimi and Jake knew it was imperative they resolve their issues. This was critical or they would never progress in Heaven. The message was clear—get with the program or be banished into the oblivion of undeveloped souls. They saw many, who refused or were not ready to progress, roaming aimlessly. So Jake and Mimi knew they were obligated to match the spouses they left behind. They were told being assigned to Marcel's support group was a privilege.

Before GPYF, they became support-group junkies since arriving in Heaven. Jake attended a gay support group and stopped when he was propositioned by a transsexual. Then he tried the disgraced bankers' group; but, since he never committed fraud on Earth, he felt out of place. Mimi went to the eating disorders group that forced everyone to eat healthy snacks. Then she attended the sex addicts' group— mainly to hear the graphic sex stories. Marcel found them both lurking around the GPYF support group gazebo and recruited them. They had no idea he was once a bad priest.

Jake wasn't sure he should go to GPYF. Why did he feel so much guilt when he wasn't Jewish? Then he did leave his wife, Samantha, in a very shitty situation.

Mimi was tired of the guilt and wearing the same black dress she died in. Matching her husband Syd on Earth was probably her only chance of getting into a new outfit. Neither Jake nor Mimi wanted to chance getting thrown into a valley of lost souls. At least they had that in common—besides being dead and hating each other.

Chapter One

GPYF

"When I lost control of all my bodily functions, Samantha was fabulous," said Jake Becker.

"That's just the sort of skill set my Sydney needs," responded Mimi Weis with an air of authority. Jake frowned. They had this discussion many times.

Jake—a tall, lanky, balding man in his mid-thirties—wore a dress shirt, slacks, and wire-rimmed glasses. He retained the demeanor of the conservative banker he was on Earth but had more edge—a Midwesterner who was shaped by the big city. Mimi, a tall, plump woman in a shapeless black dress, looked older than her thirty-two years. She postured herself as she did in her younger, better-looking days on Earth and batted her eyes a lot. She spoke with the distinct New York Jewish accent of her era.

Jake and Mimi's conversations of late took a nastier tone. Mimi had a bad habit of hanging onto Jake's arm when talking.

"You have a poor track record for your old Syd," said Jake, shaking Mimi's arm off him.

"I take offense at that comment," Mimi shot back.

"I was Syd's soul mate. I can feel that Samantha is too."

"Whoa," Jake said, raising his palms. "Why would I want a repeat for my Samantha of being a caregiver with no benefits? Syd's finances are a disaster."

"Sydney's having a temporary financial setback. He'll turn it around, with Samantha's help."

"So Samantha is to be Syd's financial rescuer *and* his nurse?" Jake flailed his arms. "Syd is twenty years older than Samantha and can provide no financial security for my family!"

"You were a fucking banker. So why did you leave them broke?" Mimi responded with her hands on her hips.

Jake turned red with anger as he looked out at the blue sky and rolling green hills through the large, open, star-shaped porticos. The breeze was warm, fresh, and smelled of lavender. Then, with a loud sigh, he regained his composure.

"Mimi, you've hounded me ever since I arrived here. I'm done." Jake turned his back and walked toward the archway of the gazebo, which housed a circular group meeting room. It was painted a meditative blue with soft green armchairs.

"Let Marcel decide," Mimi yelled. "He's the group leader."

Jake turned around and yelled back, "Marcel promised Samantha would end up with the right soul mate and I'm holding him to it."

"It's not a given that our spouses are guaranteed a better life because we're riddled with guilt," Mimi responded.

"That's why your beloved Sydney keeps ending up with losers, tramps, and gold diggers."

"Time's running out for Syd," Mimi yelled. "Where are you going? It's time for group!"

Marcel entered the gazebo and watched the heated interchange.

"Selfish bitch!" said Jake while walking away.

"Stubborn asshole!" Mimi screamed back.

"Can we be nice to each other? This *is* Heaven, after all," Marcel said, raising his eyebrows.

Marcel worked with Mimi ever since she arrived in her shapeless housedress. Bewildered by her sudden departure from Earth, she was unsettled for a long time. Her attempts to console her earthly husband, Syd, and her little son, Damien, from the spirit world only caused them more grief. They were lost souls on Earth and she begged Marcel to help find Syd a new wife.

At first Mimi was picky and only wanted someone she knew or had an earthly connection to. "Why would I match my Syd up with a stranger?" Mimi would say. She was also adamant her son be raised by a Jewish woman. Mimi's fear was that Syd would end up with a *shiksa* who would turn her son into a *goy*. Worse was the idea that Syd would be happy with a *shiksa*. So many misfires of matching him up with friends, neighbors of friends, cousins of friends, and a poor Russian immigrant. She finally conceded to the notion of opening her horizons and considering a non-Jewish woman for Syd.

Marcel pointed out that as Syd aged, he was attracted to

shiksas. He made her realize the failure to find Syd a peaceful life fueled her guilt and inability to move on in the spirit world.

"Do you realize why you are dressed as you were when you left Earth?" Marcel asked Mimi.

"I can't move on until I find my boys peace," Mimi cried. "It's because of me they've been miserable."

"They have their own free will on Earth. Syd had choices because you insisted I keep throwing women in front of him."

"You could have said 'no'," Mimi said.

"So now blame me," Marcel retorted.

Marcel took Mimi's hands in his. "It's time to let go. Syd's up there in Earth years and you need to decide."

"I know," Mimi whimpered.

"As for Damien, you know where that's leading and it's out of your hands."

"Stop! Stop!" Mimi jumped up and put her hands to her ears.

Marcel took her hand, led her back to the cushy sofa, and sat her down. He tugged at the hem of her garment.

"That dress won't come off until you're ready, hon."

"Then can I wear anything I want?" she asked in a little voice.

"Of course, doll! You've seen the heavenly wardrobe department. It's an array of clothing from all ages. You can dress ancient Egyptian, Greek, Roman, Renaissance, or Civil War style; like a suffragette, a flapper, a bobby-soxer, or a Republican. Cross-dress if you want. No one will stop you."

Mimi laughed.

Marcel continued, "There are non-earthly fashions from those planets which exploded and dumped their hand-me-downs into the atmosphere." Marcel got serious. "You have to get your shit together. Find Syd a decent woman with a good heart who will love him until he dies."

Mimi sat up and raised her hand. "Get Jake to agree to match Syd with his wife."

Marcel looked puzzled. "Samantha's not a Jew."

"I don't care. If you think she's a good match for Syd, then I agree."

"Let me talk to Jake first." Marcel patted her thigh and left her alone. He wandered outside the gazebo, looking for Jake.

Marcel found him sitting in a lotus position on a lawn,

meditating. Jake shifted around, unable to find a comfortable position.

"You're restless," noted Marcel in a soft voice.

"It's that pain in the ass, Mimi, who gets to me every time."

Marcel sat down next to Jake in a lotus position and said, "Let me help you release the guilt and the shame."

Jake turned to Marcel, looking puzzled.

"Shame? Why do you say that?"

"Guilt for leaving your wife and child in those conditions?" Marcel asked with his eyes closed and his palms out. He added, "I think you want to do it all over again, but differently."

"If I had the chance, I would tell Samantha how much I loved her. I would shower her and Bobby with my love right to the end, instead of ignoring them."

Marcel shifted, opened his eyes, turned to Jake, and asked, "What if I told you it was possible?"

"To go back down and relive my life?"

"Not exactly," Marcel responded. "You can find another man for Samantha and speak all your love and devotion through him. That's all I can offer."

Jake nodded. "Sold. Better than nothing."

Marcel rose, took Jake by the hand, and led him back to the meeting room. Mimi was still sitting on the sofa. Marcel motioned to them to reconcile. They reluctantly shook hands and took their seats. A clock chimed and Marcel signaled it was time for group.

The support group members filed into the room, including Carmella Santini. She appeared as if a gust of wind propelled her from behind. Carmella, a stocky, petite, fiery, and feisty platinum blonde with a heavy New Jersey accent, was known on Earth as "The Seaside Psychic." She wore a flowered pant suit, wedged heels, and smelled of cheap perfume.

Carmella departed Earth after a bout with breast cancer, leaving behind a truck mechanic husband, Frank, and a young, spoiled daughter, Annabelle.

Marcel acknowledged a new recruit in the group, a young man in fatigues. He asked everyone to make introductions and motioned for Jake to begin.

"I'm Jake, and I left Samantha and little Bobby in 1994."

Marcel then nodded towards Mimi.

"Mimi. 1974. Left behind Sydney and five-year-old Damien."

Carmella piped up. "Details! What's wrong with youse guys? Let me start out by telling you about my boobies."

Jake rolled his eyes. The young man in fatigues chuckled.

Carmella used hand gestures as she spoke and held her breasts.

"They were gorgeous—not too small, not too big, and nipples to die for."

"Are we going to hear the story again about the famous plastic surgeon who felt you up?" Mimi asked.

Carmella ignored Mimi's comment and continued, "My Frank won a trifecta at the track and said, 'Take this dough and buy new tits.' I was fucking floored."

Carmella adjusted herself in her chair and crossed her legs.

"For fifteen years, he never complained about my boobs." She uncrossed her legs and crossed them again.

Jake looked bored and offered the young man in fatigues a stick of gum.

Chewing loudly, the new recruit said in a heavy Southern accent, "I think ah'm in the wrong group, y'all." He sat up and continued speaking in his thick drawl, "I caught my wife fucking my buddy when I was home on leave, so I fucked her sister."

Carmella piped up, "The cheating spouses' group meets on Thursdays, three floors below here. I heard that room is hot as hell." She threw her head back in a belly laugh.

Jake asked Marcel casually, "What if you cheat, die, and leave the spouse with small children? Which group are you in?"

Marcel turned to the new member and said, "Your wife was pregnant."

"What the fuck?" the young man responded.

Mimi piped up, "That's a double whammy."

The new recruit shot up out of his chair.

"I don't fucking believe you, dude. It probably ain't mine. She was a whore."

Marcel extended his palms out to the new guy and, in a calming voice, said, "Share your story, soldier."

Jake interjected, "Start with your name and when you died."

The soldier circled the group like an animal and tried to light a cigarette.

Mimi cleared her throat and reminded him, "You can't smoke up here."

"What are they gonna do? Throw me out?." Then he laughed at his own joke and threw the cigarette out of the portico.

"*Oy vey,* isn't there a fine, like spiritual demerits, for throwing a lit cigarette?" Mimi asked.

"My name is Bishop...Bishop Leatherberry. I died on December 13, 2003, during Operation Red Dawn and been wanderin' round here ever since."

Jake perked up and asked, "The capture of Saddam Hussein?"

Carmella looked impressed.

"I like to keep up with events down there," Jake proudly said.

"Yes, sirree. They reported no lives lost, but that's bullshit. I was killed by a sniper in a nearby village." Bishop took a deep breath. "They wanted a clean operation; looks better on the evening news."

Mimi asked Bishop, "Who did you leave behind?"

Bishop stood up and cleared his throat. "Mah darlin' wife. Velma was humping my buddy, Willy 'Fathead' Fitzsimmons. Jesus Christ Almighty, you go off to war and tell a buddy to take care of your wife and he does it with his dick."

He then remarked, "Where is that dude at? Jesus, I mean. I thought he'd be one of the good ole boys, talking up a storm."

Mimi piped up, "He's got a new look—cut his hair and shaved his beard. I reminded him that he was a Jew before he turned into a *goy.*"

Carmella was appalled. "Jesus? I love that guy. He was a Jew?"

Jake laughed. "Mimi's right. Jesus was born a Jew and killed by them too. I heard he changed his name to Bob. Too much baggage being called Jesus."

"Not only is he a Jew, but he's a little darker than you think." Mimi said.

Jake asked, grinning, "Is his skin darker than a paper bag?"

Carmella made an angry face and uttered, "Holy Christ! I mean, Holy Bob!"

Bishop piped up, "I don't give a rat's ass if Jesus looks like a sand nigger. Can I get answers please about my whore wife?"

Carmella whispered to Jake, "What's a sand nigger?"

Jake whispered back, "A Muslim, I think."

"I get it. Dark people in the desert, right?" Carmella smiled, proud that she figured it out.

Marcel raised his hand and said to Bishop, "We'll see in the viewing room if Velma had your kid or Fathead Fitzsimmons'."

Bishop took out a cigarette from his shirt pocket and stuck it in his mouth without lighting it.

"Jesus is really a darky, huh? This is one fucked-up place. Every time I try to find out about Velma, all I hear is, 'Ya not ready, Bishop, more spiritual growth, Bishop.' Might as well send me back to Earth as an itty-bitty slug—lowest animal on the food chain."

Carmella crossed and uncrossed her legs. "I just want to get back down there and finish business."

Mimi asked, "Why are people so anxious to get back down there? It is delightful here. Equality, no unemployment, no wars, crises, or famines."

Jake added, "No fucked-up kids to make you miserable."

Mimi smirked at Jake.

Carmella got feisty. "Nuthin' happens up here. You can't shop, eat, or fuck."

"Well said," noted Jake.

"I've been wanting to get my nails and my roots done since I died," Carmella said as she held out her hands and then pointed to her hair.

Marcel stood and walked over to Bishop, who looked troubled. He laid a hand on his shoulder.

"Son, I know Heaven isn't what you thought it would be," said Marcel.

Jake looked towards Bishop and weighed in. "Confused, unhappy, and angry people in transition."

Marcel chimed in, "You must have made progress, soldier. You're here." He pointed to the group. "We're getting off track; follow me to the viewing room. We have work to do."

Mimi motioned for Jake to speak to Marcel.

"You promised next time we were in the viewing room, you would attend to our spouses," Jake said firmly to Marcel.

"You both have been the biggest pains in the ass," Marcel said, directing his words to Jake and Mimi. "You've been around for ages, your spouses are in a mess, and I'm tired of your bickering."

"Mimi's the goddamn problem," said Jake loudly. "She wants to hook my Samantha up with an old man."

Mimi stood up with her hands on her hips. "*No one* is good enough for Samantha. What is she? Fucking royalty?"

"Simmer down. I've had enough," Marcel said. "Age? Money? Irrelevant. It's their soul path and the compatibility meter that matter. We'll settle whether Syd and Samantha should be matched in Heaven."

Jake and Mimi were about to go at it again, but Marcel raised his hand to stop them. He almost suggested that their earthly spouses might not find their soul mates in their present lifetimes. They might be forced to cope with their guilt. Marcel bit his tongue, took a deep breath, and thought, *Patience.* He needed an easy match and low-hanging fruit, so he decided to fix Bishop's spouse first and hoped Jake and Mimi wouldn't kill each other in the meantime.

Then Marcel chuckled to himself, "They're already dead."

Chapter Two

The Viewing Room

The viewing room was in an adjoining structure to the support group area. It was an open-air theater with several rows of comfy white leather seats and drink holders. There was a large movie screen at the front and a wider chair that swiveled so Marcel could face the support-group members.

Once a group member was ready to match their earthly spouse, Marcel would take them into the viewing room. They would review potential matches using a compatibility meter, known as CM, which flashed on the screen. Once a potential match was found and the guilty spouses agreed, Marcel would facilitate the meeting of the couple on Earth.

Marcel's track record in matchmaking recently became inconsistent and he felt he had lost the magic touch. Who could he confide in that he was burning out?

It was becoming routine and sometimes he disregarded low compatibility scores just to move on. He hoped Carmella would be a good addition to the group and help him. As "The Seaside Psychic," she read the dead from Earth; now, in Heaven, she read the living.

"My Frank needs a good match," Carmella insisted. "He's getting real antsy and he's about to sleep with the neighborhood tramp!"

"Not your turn," Marcel said without looking at her.

"What is this? A friggin' bakery? Did you pass out numbahs?"

While entertaining, Carmella was sometimes very disruptive.

The group settled into the comfy white home-theater chairs, forming a circle. Marcel pointed a laser on Bishop and grabbed a remote control. An image appeared on the screen.

He zoomed right in on an image of Bishop running through an Iraqi village with a machine gun. He looked intently at himself. When Marcel froze the scene, Bishop noticed the sniper on a rooftop in the corner of the image.

"That rag-head bugger!" Bishop yelled. "I coulda blown him away—easy."

Carmella blurted out, "I betcha nuthin' good became of him."

Jake shook his head. "He probably became a general in the Iraqi Army."

Marcel proceeded with a view of Bishop's life before the shooting. They watched Bishop enlisting in the army, his farewell party, and kissing his wife good-bye before deployment. Velma, a lanky, stringy-haired blonde, was shaken as they embraced.

Marcel moved to the scene of Bishop's private chat with his buddy. Fathead Fitzsimmons was an obese man who promised to look after Velma.

Marcel fast-forwarded to Velma getting the news of Bishop's death from two soldiers at her front door and falling into the arms of Willy Fitzsimmons.

Velma is visibly pregnant and crying, *"I'm gonna have a dead man's baby!"*

Marcel made the image larger. Bishop was rattled. He stood, paced the room, and covered his eyes.

"That bitch could have told me," Bishop yelled. Then, calming down, he asked meekly, "Boy or girl?" Then he got angry again. "How did she know it was mine?"

Marcel insisted Bishop continue watching and ordered him to sit down. In the next image, Willy Fitzsimmons falls awkwardly to his knees, proposing marriage to Velma, who holds a baby. *"I want the little bugger to have a daddy. It's what Bishop would've wanted. Marry me, Velma."*

Bishop looked disgusted and then questioned Marcel, "So, why am I in this group if Velma, my baby, and the fathead live like three peas in a goddamn pod?"

Jake piped up, "Something tells me it didn't work out that way. Right, Marcel?"

Marcel forwarded to another scene of Willy Fitzsimmons committing an armed robbery of a gas station and getting shot dead by the owner.

"Son of a bitch!" screamed Bishop. "That stupid fathead!

Where is the *hell* is he? Or should I say where the heaven is he?"

Carmella, Jake and Mimi laughed while Marcel was serious.

"So you see, the door is open to find a match for Velma and a daddy for your boy." Marcel handed an envelope to Bishop.

Bishop looked puzzled. Marcel flashed the number 99.9 on the ceiling and announced like a tabloid talk-show host, "Bishop Leatherberry. You *are* the baby's father. 99.9 percent probability."

Bishop took the envelope and walked out of the room and into the night.

Marcel said loudly, "When you're ready to work on a match, I'm available."

He brought up the image of Velma and Willy Fitzsimmons and hit a button on his CM remote.

It flashed "200: marginal."

"Just curious," said Marcel as he switched off the image and number.

Mimi stood up. "I've been asking you to attend to my Syd for ages. How come soldier boy gets preferential treatment?"

An impatient Carmella said, "Wait your turn. Marcel made it clear you and Jake are pains in the ass."

Marcel turned to Carmella. "Okay, Seaside Psychic, you're up."

Carmella stood erect and opened her arms. "Jeez, finally. Bring it on, chief."

Marcel held the remote up and began with an image of Carmella on a poster: 'Live tonight: The Seaside Psychic and The Spirit Connection.'

Mimi added, "Could be a rock group: Carmella and The Spirit Connections."

"Hate that photo! A smiling mushroom head," lamented Carmella, while adjusting her hair. She added, "Look how chubby I was. That was before the chemo."

"You aren't exactly a stick now," Mimi remarked.

Marcel forwarded to the image of Carmella on stage, addressing the audience.

"How much did they pay to see you?" Jake asked Carmella.

Carmella responded, "I think it was two for one or a Groupon."

The Seaside Psychic sat on a high stool, in a tight red

pantsuit with flashy, sparkly jewelry, and holding a microphone. She spoke with an intimate tone.

"Your departed loved ones are in a peaceful place with people they care about."

Jake and Mimi groaned. Marcel interjected, "Shut up, you two," and returned to the image of Carmella.

"They have no worries, no pain, and no guilt. They are free spirits," Carmella continued.

They heard Bishop cursing outside the viewing room.

The image showed Carmella hopping off the stool and walking down the stairs from the stage, into the audience.

"Someone is coming through." Carmella, holding a microphone, stops in front of a row of women and addresses a thirty-something woman.

"Did your grandmother just pass?" Carmella puts the microphone in the woman's face, waiting for her response.

The woman tears up and says, "Yes".

Carmella puts her hand on her arm and says, "She's fine and she loves you."

Suddenly, Carmella is entranced by something else in the next row. She leans over to another woman and says, "I love that handbag. Where did you get it?"

The woman holds up a gold lamé bag and responds, "Online."

Carmella touches the bag and says, "It's sexy. Wait! Did a young man just pass in your family?"

The woman nods and says, "Yes, my brother."

Carmella speaks into the microphone softly, "He's at peace, no longer in pain."

The woman tears up and thanks Carmella, who gives her a hug.

Carmella touches the handbag again with one finger as if it's burning hot. The audience laughs.

Marcel froze the image of Carmella and said, "Carmella, you were drawn to this woman for another reason? High CM with Frank."

Marcel hit the remote and an image of Carmella's husband, smiling in a T-shirt and cap. Carmella jumped up and tried to hug and kiss the 3-D image.

Marcel motioned for her to sit down. He then flashed the woman with the gold lamé handbag next to Frank. He turned on his CM meter remote and it flashed "500: excellent."

Carmella shot up out of her chair and paced the room.

"Who the fuck is she? Why would she be good for my Frank?" She flailed her arms and pointed to the image of the woman. "She doesn't look Italian. In fact, her eyes look a little slanty."

Jake groaned and said, "Here we go."

Mimi remarked to Marcel, "And you thought *I* was a pain in the ass?"

Marcel turned the images off and addressed the group.

"Carmella, you're obviously not ready for this."

Carmella stood at the doorway. "I think I'll go outside with soldier boy and look for Jesus with the makeover."

Marcel shook his head and said, "Now is not the time to hunt down Jesus 2.0. We have work to do."

He walked over, took Carmella's hand, and then yelled out the doorway, "Come on back, Bishop. We need you in here."

As Marcel guided Carmella back to her seat, Bishop lumbered in and hoisted himself onto the portico sill. He clearly didn't want to sit with the group. Marcel took his seat and picked up the remote.

Marcel turned to Mimi and firmly said, "Okay, one last shot. If you get this wrong, Syd will leave the Earth a very unhappy and lonely soul."

Marcel held up the remote and started with an image of Syd, a bald, robust seventy-year-old, looking energetic and distinguished. He was shown flirting with a young office assistant. Then he did a fast reverse and pulled up Syd's failed relationships. He stopped the viewing and calculated the CM with each woman, which ranged from adequate to poor. The number flashed above the images. Mimi was embarrassed, as she had agreed to each match.

Jake interjected, "As I said, bad track record."

Mimi gave him the finger. She also painfully watched her son, grow up and become more hostile with each new woman Syd brought into his life. Marcel stopped the reverse view when he reached Mimi's death.

The group watched her slump to the floor, wearing the same dress she wore in the viewing room.

Five-year-old Damien throws a glass of water at her, trying to wake her up. He shouts, "Stop playing dead, Mommy." Then Marcel reversed to the scene just before Mimi's sudden death, when Damien yells, "I hate you!"

"That's really sad, Mimi," said Jake. "Boohoo."

Carmella took it literally, blurting out, "Jake, you're a regular Heckle and Jyde."

Everyone looked puzzled, but Marcel corrected her, "It's Jekyll and Hyde, honey."

"So, I'm not educated like youse guys," Carmella responded.

Marcel stopped the images and faced Mimi, who was now in tears.

"Miriam Weis..." Marcel said with a piercing look.

Mimi interrupted him, "I couldn't control my own son. Syd couldn't cope either."

"What if I told you no one could have helped your boy?"

Mimi cried. Marcel rose up and put his arms around her shoulders. "I get it. You want to make it up to Syd by giving him true love."

Jake stood up. "Why does my Samantha have to be the savior?"

Marcel hit the remote and produced a view of Samantha and Syd side by side. Then he grabbed the other remote and the CM showed up on the ceiling. The number >1000 and lights flashing with sparks appeared simultaneously.

"That's why," Marcel said, pointing the laser to the number on the ceiling. "That means off the charts. Fucking powerful. Doesn't happen often."

Mimi blurted out, pointing to Jake, "This horse's ass won't agree to the match."

It wasn't a given, Marcel explained. "To consummate the match, Samantha and Syd need to have entered each other's orbit at some point on Earth."

Mimi shifted nervously. "So show us if it happened, already."

"It had to happen at least once. Let's find out," Marcel said.

Marcel hit the remote and images kept appearing. He forwarded and reversed through images and years, waiting for a signal. A buzzer sounded, and he freeze-framed a tall, forty-something Syd with square dark-rimmed glasses and seventies-style haircut, wearing a suit, and carrying a briefcase. Samantha appeared as an awkward teen with glasses and braces, wearing a floppy hat.

Marcel gleefully announced, "I found it. 1976. Here is where Syd and Samantha entered each other's orbit. Syd's office was a mile from Samantha's high school and this diner."

Marcel hit the remote, and there was a visual of Syd telling a joke to a group of teenage girls, including Samantha, in a diner. The girls are giggling. Samantha looks at Syd as if he is a boring businessman. Samantha and Syd exchange a quick glance without the conscious knowledge they will meet again decades later under entirely different circumstances.

Marcel fast-forwarded to an older Syd, with receding hairline and a paunch. Then he placed an image of Samantha as a beautiful young woman with long dark hair and yearning in her eyes.

"Ten years after, in 1984—Mimi, I offered you Samantha. But you wanted only Jewish women for Syd so, he ended up with this."

Marcel held the remote and froze an image of an overly made-up, buxom blonde woman sitting on Syd's lap.

Carmella laughed. "Who the fuck is that?"

Mimi replied, "*Oy!* She's my cousin Sara's neighbor. *That* was a mistake."

Bishop said, "Looks like the Tijuana hooker who popped my cherry!"

Then Marcel put up a visual of Samantha and Jake side by side. He held his laser pointer to the ceiling, flashing the CM of 700.

"Jake was the next best match for Samantha," Marcel said.

Jake choked up. "You mean you matched us, Marcel?"

Marcel hadn't but wanted to take credit. He continued showing a visual diary. He ran through Jake and Samantha's romantic journey and then their wedding. Jake and Carmella got emotional.

Bishop was touched. "I wish I had one-tenth of that kind'a romance. How did it end?"

"Tragically and entirely my fault," Jake said, burying his head in his hands.

Chapter Three

Jake and Samantha

Jake lay in bed with a high fever, coughing violently and frequently. It was 1992 and he was diagnosed with full-blown AIDS.

He sobbed uncontrollably as the parade of Doctors left the room. They strongly suggested that Samantha and their young son get tested as soon as possible.

A mortified Samantha turned to Jake and blurted out, "Maybe you die first, then me, and then Bobby."

Samantha peered out into the hall, hoping they were not really in a hospital and that she was just dreaming. The activity in the corridor looked too real. She would have to deal with the possibility that they, including their one-year-old son, would all die from AIDS. She also thought it was very unfair.

Many of her girlfriends fucked their brains out until 1985, banging multiple guys at parties with no condoms without consequences. Samantha, after only two sex partners in her life contracted a killer STD.

Samantha wondered how Jake, a senior vice-president of a major international bank, a father, a husband, and a devotee of an Indian guru, could end up with the mother of all STDs. The hospital staff also wondered.

Jake vehemently denied any high-risk behavior associated with HIV infection. He became very snobbish when he was moved to the wing occupied by drug addicts, hookers, and homosexuals. He resented being associated with these types and rarely spoke to them.

As the AIDS patients roamed the hallways in various stages of illness, he would yell from his bed, "I'm not one of them!"

Alone in the hospital room at night, Jake would sob—powerless and riddled with guilt. He secretly hoped he wouldn't wake up and that he had the strength to end it. The thought of being responsible for Samantha and their baby son becoming sick with AIDS was overwhelming. He avoided the subject and hoped he wouldn't live much longer.

The Doctors recommended that Jake get counseling. He was appalled.

"Imagine," he said to Samantha haughtily, "they want me to see a shrink."

Samantha was tempted to spell out the situation but kept her comments to herself.

You're probably a closet homosexual and may have passed a deadly STD to your wife and child...and you think you don't need counseling?

Jake's older brother went to counseling and attended an AIDS support group in an effort to cope with what he called his brother's 'death sentence'.

Samantha was a romantic and believed in miracles. She tried to keep Jake's spirits up. "We'll get through this, Jake. I'll do anything to help you get better."

Jake's response was a request to bring him *vibhuti*—the sacred ash he was given by an Indian guru. Samantha knew what he planned to do. She had no idea how to explain to the nurses why Jake smeared dried cow shit on his forehead. She was already sneaking in vitamins, but dried cow shit was something else.

Jake and Samantha avoided talking about the disease, and the unthinkable—that all three of them faced illness and may-be death at the same time.

The nurses and Doctors pounded Samantha daily. "We'll test you right now if you like."

One nurse grabbed Samantha's arm and said, "Get tested so you can stop thinking about it."

"I'm not thinking about it. All my energies are focused on my husband," Samantha responded to the nurse.

"If we are HIV positive, what can you do for us? People are dying with or without the new drug, AZT." She then waved an article from the underground press in the air.

Neither she nor little Bobby had any symptoms. She would take the gamble.

Jake didn't voice an opinion either way on the subject. But he had a lot to say about the hospital food.

"This food will kill me first," he said while holding up a dry piece of chicken.

"Taste it," he insisted.

She shook her head. "No thanks. I believe you. But if you don't gain some weight they'll put you on a feeding tube."

Along with home-cooked meals she brought Bobby along to cheer him up. Since Jake was considered terminal, they allowed a small child to visit.

Bobby, at eighteen months, found the hospital a curious place. One minute, he was at Jake's bedside, and the next, he wandered the hallway. Samantha found Bobby in the next door room talking gibberish to a comatose white-haired patient. Then Samantha realized the woman was not comatose but dead. An orderly came in and pulled a white sheet over the body.

Samantha took Bobby's hand and let him out of the room. "Come, that lady is having a nice long rest."

Jake was visited by a plethora of Doctors and residents. They all had different messages and different advice.

"Don't worry; you'll live a long life," Jake would say, imitating the Doctors.

Then there was the clinical trial squad that tried to persuade him to join a double-blind study. Jake refused after a young resident whispered in his ear, "I wouldn't, if I were you," alluding to the fact that if you actually got the drug, it could kill you faster than the disease.

Samantha wasn't going to let Jake go without a fight. She researched, in a pre-Internet era, treatments and experimental cures. She would burst into his hospital room with news from the latest article she read or person she had talked to.

"There are new drugs coming," Samantha said one day in excitement.

Jake pretended to be interested, but deep down he knew it was futile.

By day, Samantha had chest pains and felt like she was falling into a deep, dark pit. At night, she dreamed of a large, slimy black creature hovering around the bed. Part of it was Jake's illness and part was their debt.

Despite being a bank vice-president, Jake was the worst personal finance manager. When Jake fell ill, Samantha discovered the extent of his debts that had accumulated after a messy divorce and custody battle over his children with his first wife.

"I can't do this!" Samantha screamed one day. "The debts,

your children, your ex-wife, Bobby, your illness. Who's going to take care of me if I get sick and who the hell is going to take care of Bobby if we both die?"

Jake remained silent.

Samantha liquidated most of their possessions. She gave away all the framed photos of the Indian guru. Jake didn't seem to mind. She handed the care of Jake's twin daughters to his ex-wife full-time and arranged for her , Jake and Bobby to move in with relatives rent-free.

Samantha fought for Jake's health and battled the Doctors, who gave her conflicting stories. She argued with Jake's ex-wife over child support payments, and tried to get Jake's daughters to help with Bobby.

Samantha also tried unsuccessfully to get Jake's family to rally. They offered little support and Jake would say, "They look at me as if I'm already dead."

Jake's fifteen-year-old twin daughters, Helen and Jana, in their naiveté treated him as if he had a bad cold. In a way, it made Jake feel normal.

Jake went to great lengths to conceal his illness. He was amused when he heard his boss sent out a warning memo about the dangers of overwork and naming him, a known workaholic, as an example of 'what not to do'.

They were almost outed when a neighbor said laughingly, "When I saw you come home from the hospital, man, I thought you had AIDS! But you're looking much better now."

Samantha and Jake laughed with the neighbor while exchanging a quick glance.

Samantha promised never to tell anyone about his illness. As Samantha lied about Jake, she protected herself and Bobby too. She feared the "AIDS family" label and the associated stigma.

Jake rallied for a few weeks, then came down with one illness after another. She begged him to hang on. Samantha felt like she was fighting the virus battle by herself. She dragged Jake to underground support groups, Doctors, and counselors. She changed his diet and fed him herbal and vitamin supplements. She found a Doctor with an alternative immune therapy potion and another who sold her black market interferon.

Jake went through the motions and pretended to be interested. The shame was engulfing him along with the disease.

After a year, Samantha finally got up the courage to ask him, "Am I healing you into life or into death?"

When he didn't respond, she knew the answer. She stopped looking for cures and remedies, and concentrated on making him comfortable. He became more withdrawn as the disease progressed. Samantha tried to draw Jake out, showing him affection, but he wouldn't react. They rarely had conversations and his interactions with little Bobby were minimal.

Bobby kept Samantha going. He needed her to be strong and pretend everything was normal. It became obvious that Bobby was the future, not Jake.

After battling the virus for eighteen months, Jake looked like a concentration camp survivor and was blind. When he felt the end was close, Jake discussed the funeral arrangements.

"I want to be cremated—a simple church service with some Mozart. Then stick me in the family crypt with the other dead Beckers."

While this sounded easy coming from Jake, Samantha shuddered at the thought of sending his body to a crematorium.

Jake tried to console her one night in bed. "Don't worry; you'll be happy when it's all over."

Samantha couldn't imagine what "happy" would feel like.

"Don't worry, you'll meet someone else," Jake said. "You're still very good-looking."

Another man was the last thing on Samantha's mind and she certainly didn't think she looked good. In fact, she was using more concealer, lotions, and potions since Jake became ill. Then there was the occasional man who chatted her up at the deli counter or a whistle from a construction worker.

Jake slept a lot and, sometimes upon waking, said there were people in the room. Samantha thought they were probably relatives from the other side. She heard of such things and took it in stride.

When Jake became too weak to get to the bathroom alone, Samantha lost her temper. "How dare you leave me broke with a child to raise alone!"

She couldn't help it; she was scared and shattered.

Jake's skin became paper-thin and he lost control of his bodily functions. As Samantha promised, she didn't move him to a hospital.

At first she tore up Bobby's pull-up diapers, and tried to make Jake feel comfortable. After a few days she couldn't do it alone and made arrangements for home care, using what little money they had left.

Jake must have known. He feared being hauled away to a facility and attached to life support.

That night, while Samantha gave Jake a sponge bath, Bobby asked to watch TV. She fed Jake warm milk with a straw and then whispered in his ear, "You've been weak before and we managed to pull through, but if you want to let go now, just let go."

A few minutes later, Jake stopped breathing. The paramedics and the police came, seized his medications and asked to see his medical records. When they saw the diagnosis, they agreed not to resuscitate.

Samantha told Bobby, "Daddy go bye-bye; give him a little kiss." He did and was led out of the room by a lady police officer while the paramedics prepared the body to be moved.

Samantha removed Jake's wedding ring and a silver chain from around his neck before they bagged him. She clutched the cup of milk, which was still warm. His soiled sheets and pajamas were still soaking in detergent. She wailed over Jake's body but regretted it later, as she read in a book about Tibetan death rituals that hysterics could delay his ascent to the other side.

* * * *

Jake hesitated as he left his body. He felt deep pain watching Samantha wail and Bobby sitting with a lady police officer. The white light beckoned and he was not turning back. Jake thought whatever was on the other side had to be better.

* * * *

Shortly after they took Jake's body away, a telemarketer called, asking if Mister Becker was available.

"You just missed him," said Samantha. She couldn't help having a moment of black humor in the middle of what felt like a surreal situation.

The next day, Samantha visited the funeral home to make arrangements for Jake's cremation. The funeral director—an obese, balding young man—showed her expensive caskets.

Samantha remarked, "But you only burn them."

"Some people want their loved ones to burn in style," said the director.

"He left us broke. I don't see cardboard as an option?" Samantha asked. The funeral director grimaced but sold her the cheapest coffin allowed by law. She also purchased a plastic urn.

Jake's instructions were to bury him with the other dead Beckers. She didn't think they would mind the plastic.

Before burial, Jake's twin daughters, Helen and Jana, stuffed notes in the urn. Samantha saw one of the notes had a cartoon figure of Jake with a bulbous nose.

* * * *

Samantha went to see The Seaside Psychic for a reading. Samantha heard her on the radio and found the phone number. The psychic had an unexpected cancellation. From her radio voice, Samantha expected some gypsy, earthy type, and not a gum-chewing, chunky, rough, boisterous woman with short blonde hair.

Carmella greeted Samantha warmly at her modest suburban home in the Jersey shore town of Seaside. Samantha was led into her living room of nondescript furniture.

Carmella held Samantha's hands and looked into her eyes. "Your husband just passed, didn't he?"

Samantha was flabbergasted and choked back tears.

"He's here, hon," Carmella said.

"Where?" Samantha asked.

Carmella waved her hands in the air, then grabbed a Kleenex from a box on her coffee table and dabbed Samantha's eyes.

"You should use waterproof mascara, hon. People will think I socked ya in the face."

Samantha was anxious to get a message from Jake. Carmella cleared her throat and became annoyed. "Yes. I hear you. Wait. I'll tell her. Jeez, he's impatient."

"What's he saying?" Samantha asked.

"He's sorry he didn't tell you how much he loved you and how grateful he is that you took care of him. He wants to come back to Earth as soon as possible to be with you."

Samantha blew her nose and asked, "Is that it?"

Carmella nodded.

"He's talking about a cross, a necklace?"

"He wore a silver cross," Samantha responded in a shaky voice.

"He says put it on," Carmella instructed.

Samantha took the silver cross and chain out of her bag.

"I'm a little reluctant. My family has a conflicted relationship with religion," Samantha said, composing herself.

"Jake says it'll help you," Carmella said.

"My grandfather was raised by a corrupt priest and was a vehement atheist," Samantha said as she put Jake's chain around her neck.

Carmella beamed, gave Samantha a hug, and then took her check for three hundred dollars. The next day Samantha put Jake's ashes in a knapsack. She boarded a plane heading to his Midwest hometown for burial. She had a hard time deciding whether to put the urn in the overhead bin or under the seat in front of her. She sat holding what was left of Jake in her arms while Bobby played with his toy cars.

Her mind raced on so many unknowns. Where and how would they live? Would she be able to find a job? Who would take care of Bobby? How would she pay back Jake's debts? Would she be dead from AIDS before Bobby went to kindergarten?

The flight attendant offered to put the knapsack with the urn in the overhead bin. Samantha handed the bag to her and hoped Jake wouldn't spill out in flight.

As the plane took off and lifted higher into the sky, Samantha had a plan.

Chapter Four

Mimi and Syd

In 1962, when Sydney Weis was honorably discharged from the army, all he wanted was a 1953 Buick Skylark convertible. Unlike his older brother who served in Korea, Syd served in peacetime at a New Mexican army base.

Murray would often sneer at Syd's military service and call it "your phony army." He never complimented Syd on achieving training officer status or on any of his other accomplishments. They were never close and always accused each other of being 'the favorite'. Their parents, whom Syd and Murray called by their first names, claimed not to have a favorite.

Estelle would say, "Favorite, *schmavrite.* You're both my sons whether I'm above or below ground." Basically, dead or alive, she vowed to love them equally.

Syd patiently waited for Murray to move out of the family home. It was imminent in 1962, as Murray was engaged to Fran, who was in a hurry to tie the knot. Estelle speculated openly that Fran was probably pregnant.

Leonard paid no attention to his wife or his sons and occupied himself running Rothman's, the family soda fountain named for Estelle's father, a Russian immigrant.

"Best egg creams in Far Rockaway, maybe all of Queens," Syd would say his entire life.

Syd maintained he had an idyllic childhood in Far Rockaway. He spent his free time riding his bike, hanging out at the soda fountain, and engaging in feeding frenzies at relatives' houses. He would bring his lunch to the beach every day in the summer. Estelle or Leonard let him run free and he ignored Murray's foul moods. Syd was completely unaffected by the family tragedy that occurred years before his birth. There was another son who was set on fire and burned to death.

Four-year-old Murray watched as a neighbor kid doused his older brother with gasoline and lit a match. David's death was ruled an accident. Estelle and Leonard were devastated and numb with grief.

Rather than bring up the story of the neighbor who was never arrested, Estelle would claim, "Our beloved David was a victim of the convicted child serial killer, Albert Fish."

It was Estelle's way of having closure to a horrific event. She would add, "We should all be satisfied already that murderer was electrocuted in 1936."

When Syd was born in 1940, Estelle tried to put the death behind her but Leonard became withdrawn and distant.

After the military, Syd attended college on the GI Bill and was interested in the new field of industrial psychology. He liked to analyze people's behavior and enjoyed telling people what to do, as he had done in the army. Syd was gregarious as a young man, to the point of sometimes being obnoxious when quizzing people on their motivations and behavior.

"I was born to be controversial." Some people found him annoying but he was popular with the girls,. outgoing and a good dancer. He was tall, not too dark, and handsome with a sparkle in his blue-green eyes.

On the weekends, he worked at Rothman's soda fountain.

"Here, put this away," Estelle would say and secretly give Syd extra cash so he could buy his Buick. When Murray found out, a running argument began about money that lasted for the next fifty years.

Syd proudly parked his blue Buick convertible outside Rothman's and watched passersby admire it. One day, as he joked with regulars, a well-dressed young woman entered the shop and sat at the counter, watching Syd make the famous Rothman's egg cream. Twenty-five-year-old Miriam "Mimi" Garber was well-proportioned, wearing a flowered dress, high heels, and a hat. She was carefully made-up and wore a beehive hairdo. Syd could smell her perfume from behind the cash register.

She wasn't shy about staring at Syd for over five minutes. Syd was curious about this woman but was too busy to talk to her. He also noticed she wore a wedding ring and looked a few years older than he. Mimi ordered an egg cream and consumed it. When she couldn't get Syd's attention, she left him a large tip of fifty cents and walked out.

The next week Mimi came in again, this time wearing a low-cut dress that exposed cleavage and a sweater over her shoulders. She ordered a hamburger and a milk shake.

As the soda fountain wasn't busy, Syd made light conversation after he served her the food.

"Live around here?" he asked.

"Weekends, with my aunt. I think she's a friend of your mother," Mimi responded.

"Who's your aunt?" Syd asked while clearing off the counter.

"Sadie Stein," Mimi said just before slurping down the rest of the shake.

Syd winced as he remembered that Sadie Stein was on Estelle's shit list for not inviting her to her son's bar mitzvah.

Syd answered politely, "I think they know each other."

It was getting to closing time at Rothman's, and Syd sent the busboy home early so he could chat in private with Mimi. He was curious and flattered that this woman pursued him however, she was clearly married.

Mimi left money on the table but lingered, putting on fresh lipstick and adjusting her hat.

"I'm going to my Aunt Sadie's; are you heading in that direction?" she asked coyly.

"I can give you a ride," Syd responded. "I have a better idea; let's walk."

Syd quickly finished closing the store as Mimi peered at all the photos on the wall. There were local high school students, local politicians posing with Leonard and Grandpa Rothman, including Mayor Fiorello La Guardia, who made a campaign stop at the soda fountain in 1933.

"This is such a wonderful neighborhood place," Mimi said.

"Grandpa Rothman opened in 1925."

Syd shut the lights off, moved towards the door, and nodded to Mimi.

Syd walked towards the boardwalk and decided to take the long way around, as he was fascinated by Mimi and wanted to know her story.

They walked in silence for a few minutes when Mimi blurted out, "I'm married but I'm not happy."

Syd was surprised by her confession but didn't respond.

Mimi continued, "I felt a connection when I saw you at my cousin's bar mitzvah."

"Impossible; we weren't invited," Syd said.

Mimi replied with a simple, "Oh."

"That's why my mother doesn't speak to your aunt Sadie."

"I must have seen you in a photo."

Mimi stopped on the boardwalk facing the sea and, without looking at Syd, announced, "I know you may think this is crazy, but I'm going to marry you as soon as I get a divorce."

Syd was flabbergasted but didn't show it. He continued walking with Mimi a few more blocks and stopped in front of her aunt's house. They shook hands.

He thought Mimi was crazy but couldn't get her out of his mind. He asked Estelle about her. It opened a floodgate of information. Estelle knew about her father's mental illness and suicide. Then there was the bad marriage she made at nineteen to an alcoholic door-to-door salesman just to anger her mother, and the number of times Mimi went to the police station to file a report against her husband. Estelle knew details about what Mimi's father wore when he hung himself. Then there was the controversy about Mimi's undergarments on her wedding day. Syd tried to stop her but Estelle continued.

"That marriage killed her mother. Dropped dead when she heard the news that he wasn't really Jewish," Estelle recounted.

"You mean the alcoholic part didn't bother her?"

"Alcoholic could be fixed, but becoming a Jew—just like that?" Estelle snapped her fingers and shook her head, adding, "Too bad. She was a lovely girl."

"Was? She *is* a lovely girl!" responded Syd.

It was at that moment Syd felt compelled to save Mimi from her loveless marriage. He was in no rush. It could wait until he finished college and saved more money.

* * * *

Mimi would come in every few weeks at closing time, and they would walk on the beach or the boardwalk, or take a ride in his convertible with the top down. She told him how she wanted to escape her tyrannical mother and the tragedy of her father's suicide when she was twelve. Mimi's mother died just after she married Mister Garber, which she attributed to bad eating and not to the shock of her bad marriage.

Syd told her about his happy childhood and love of the

beach. They had much in common: movies, books, music. They both loved to dance.

Syd often asked her, "Why are you attracted to me?"

Mimi had a laundry list of attributes and he relished hearing them.

About a year after Syd met Mimi, a man in a cheap suit and a salesman's sample case walked into Rothman's. He approached the counter, looked at Syd, and flashed a document. Syd only saw the title, "Divorce Decree," before the man, who was Mimi's now ex-husband, stuffed the paper away in his case.

"She's all yours, pal. Lots of luck," he said. He turned around and left.

Syd ignored the warning and chalked it up to unreliable words coming from an alcoholic. He was probably a smart guy before he became a drunk. It was a relief, as Syd always feared Mimi's husband would sock him in the jaw one day.

Syd went out the next day and bought Mimi an engagement ring. On their next beach walk, he proposed and gave her the ring. Mimi was elated and eager to set a date. She wanted desperately to be Mrs. Sydney Weis, quit her job as a telephone operator, and set up house. Syd had one big caveat.

"I want you all to myself, Mimi. No kids," Syd said adamantly. He wanted her full attention forever and didn't want children interfering in their happiness. Mimi agreed, but secretly she was convinced she could change his mind.

While Syd finished college, Mimi moved in with her aunt full-time to be closer to Syd. Estelle was forced to make peace with Sadie, who finally apologized for not inviting her to the bar mitzvah, blaming her paltry finances. Estelle never bought it, as Sadie coughed up enough money for Syd and Mimi's wedding at the country club.

"For a big wedding, she has; inviting us to a little bar mitzvah, she hasn't," remarked Estelle.

Syd found a job selling windows and doors and threw himself into his work. He became a modestly successful salesman. He allowed Mimi to quit her job and hired a housekeeper.

They ate out often, as Mimi didn't like to cook. They went out dancing every Saturday night and to the movies. Mimi would bring up the subject of children once in a while, but Syd never budged. He remained steadfast: no kids.

Mimi spent her time studying design magazines and

redecorating their small apartment often. She vowed to have "coordinated color schemes in every corner."

She became frustrated. All her girlfriends were married and having their second child. She started gaining weight. Syd, who was always proud of her figure, was not pleased as she steadily went from one dress size to another. She became unappealing to him and he was vocal about it. He stopped having sex with her.

Mimi heard of a new weight-loss treatment using hypnosis. Syd reluctantly agreed to pay the exorbitant fifty-dollar fee per treatment.

"As long I get you back the way I met you," Syd said.

Mimi traveled to Manhattan once a week to see a hypnotist, Doctor Stern, who had offices in a Greenwich Village studio. She felt transformed in his presence. He was a middle-aged hipster with a beard who listened to jazz. He didn't think she was that overweight but agreed losing a few pounds wouldn't hurt.

Their sessions became intense and dealt with issues other than weight loss. Doctor Stern heard about her first failed marriage and her problems with Syd. Her longing for a child, according to Stern, was the route of her weight gain. In his professional opinion, more sex was required so she would feel like a woman again and become more fertile. After several months of treatments that went beyond hypnosis, Stern counseled her to give Syd an ultimatum.

On their fifth wedding anniversary, Mimi announced to Syd, "I want a baby—with or without you."

Syd wasn't alarmed. Maybe he neglected her; she had lost weight and he wanted to encourage her. He reluctantly agreed. To Syd's surprise, she became pregnant rather quickly. Mimi stopped seeing Doctor Stern.

Mimi put out of her mind the question of who had impregnated her, as it really didn't matter. She would have her baby, which was most important. Syd was a selfish narcissist and she would have the family and lifestyle she wanted and deserved.

Seven months later, Mimi gave birth to a large baby boy whom they named Edgar for Mimi's late father, in the Jewish tradition of naming babies after dead relatives. Syd was alarmed as Edgar had ended his days in an insane asylum. Mimi suggested they call their son by his middle name,

Damien. Years later, Syd often remarked, "The kid was doomed—named after a suicide grandfather and then the devil child in *The Omen*."

Syd warmed to the idea of having a son. He pushed Damien in a big pram along the boardwalk, the proud papa. Mimi was overjoyed but worn out from the sleepless nights.

"Syd, I can't take it!" Mimi whined. "I need help."

Syd hired a baby nurse and a cleaning lady who came twice a week. Mimi couldn't complain anymore. She had everything she wanted.

He was proud of his little family and invited Murray and Fran over to dinner when Damien was six months old. Syd showed off photos of the baby, their ocean view, Mimi's décor, and the spotless kitchen.

He said, "My wife will never wash a floor."

Mimi made things worse by commenting on Fran's chapped hands and recommending a hand lotion.

Fran and Murray kept quiet but were burning with anger. During dinner Murray hit Syd up for Estelle's upkeep. After Leonard's death, Estelle treated both sons as surrogate husbands, alternating her focus depending on how financially successful they were. Murray was a successful stockbroker on Wall Street. Although Murray made three times Syd's salary, he felt Syd should contribute equally.

Mimi was enraged and said so out loud. Murray and Fran left in the middle of dinner and didn't speak to Syd for the next fifteen years.

Syd soon made enough money to buy a modest house just before Damien turned two. Damien never left the terrible twos. He made their lives hell with tantrums and fits. Mimi took Damien to Doctor Stern. The doctor tried everything, including trying to hypnotize the toddler.

"Watch the ball swing, Damien," said Stern to the two-year-old. But Damien only kicked Stern in the shins. The kid also turned over a coffee table, breaking an expensive porcelain vase. Mimi left, extremely embarrassed.

The little boy, who looked angelic in pictures, rarely smiled or laughed and hated being touched. He was, however, a very smart little boy and taught himself to read by age four.

Syd was very proud of his son and had him perform for visitors by making him read from the classics or poetry. Invariably, Damien wouldn't finish the passage. He would throw the book at Syd and erupt in a tantrum. Syd chalked it up to "a strong will and opinion. That's my boy! "

Just before he entered kindergarten, Damien threatened to put Mimi's head in the toilet bowl and drown her. When Syd found out, he made an appointment with a child psychologist against Mimi's wishes. She feared that Damien was following in the footsteps of her father, who had long battled mental illness before his suicide.

One morning after he had a tantrum, Damien settled down, playing with his toy cars in front of the TV. He fiddled with the TV dials when Mimi pushed him away, as it was time for her favorite soap, *One Life to Live*. He slapped her and went back to his toy cars.

She sat on the sofa in her shapeless black housedress and, just as the first commercial break came, she felt woozy, grasped the back of her neck, then her forehead. All went black as she slid to the floor.

Damien looked up and yelled, "Get up, Mommy."

She didn't respond.

He repeated several times, "Wake up!"

She didn't move. He took his glass of half-finished juice and threw it over her head, and then went back playing with his toy cars. Soon after, the housekeeper let herself in and found Mimi unconscious. She called an ambulance and then Syd, who rushed to the hospital from the office. When he arrived, Mimi was DOA.

When he saw Mimi's lifeless body, Syd thought of how his father told Estelle he loved her just before he dropped dead. Syd vowed he would die in love when it was his time.

Chapter Five

The Negotiation

In the viewing room, Marcel clicked off the remote and swiveled his chair towards Jake and Mimi. They were both visibly shaken after a run-through of their respective Earth journeys with Samantha and Syd.

"You both have a lot of regrets, unfinished business," Marcel said casually.

Mimi sat upright and announced, "If you ask me, Jake was a bigger asshole than me."

"Since when did this become a pissing contest?" Jake asked.

"I should get special treatment for my Syd. I've been here longer," Mimi responded.

"Life on Earth isn't fucking fair and same goes here," Jake said. "Right, Marcel?"

Marcel cleared his throat and was about to speak when Mimi jumped in.

"At least I didn't leave anyone destitute with a deadly disease!"

"You fucked your doctor, had his baby, and didn't tell your husband. Then left him with a sick, bastard kid to raise who is not his," Jake said.

"Could have been Syd's," Mimi said.

Jake shot back, "Get real, Mimi."

Marcel intervened. "This is not productive. At this rate, you both will end up angry, lost, and guilty souls. Believe me—you don't want to go there."

"Isn't that where they put you first?" Jake asked Marcel.

"I redeemed myself," Marcel responded. "For the record, Mimi, here's the doctor and here's Damien."

Marcel flashed a photo of them side by side. Doctor Stern and Damien were unmistakably father and son. Marcel, in

Angela Page

his tabloid talk-show host voice, announced, "Doctor Stern is Damien's father!"

Mimi looked ashamed.

Jake then asked Marcel, "So, where do we go from here?"

"I want to get out of this fucking old dress and move on," Mimi whined.

Marcel leaned back in his chair and smoothed his goatee. "Are you prepared to release your spouses and accept whatever comes?"

Jake stood up and paced. "I feel guilty, ashamed, and sorry for not telling her what she meant to me. I want to make it right."

"At least we agree on something," Mimi said in a conciliatory manner.

Marcel became serious. "I repeat. Are you both prepared?"

"What the hell, I mean what the heaven, are you talking about?" Jake demanded.

Marcel grabbed the remote and shot a view of Samantha and Syd side by side, flashing the CM of over 1,000. "You both don't get it," Marcel said.

"Get what? They're compatible. I see," Mimi said.

Jake looked up and stared at Samantha, holding back tears.

Marcel then tapped the remote again, put up a visual of Syd and Mimi together, and flashed the CM number 500. Then he switched the view to Jake and Samantha and flashed 700.

Jake raised his arms and announced, "I get it."

Mimi looked puzzled. "Get what? Is this a riddle?"

Jake turned to Mimi and asked, "Don't you see what Marcel is trying to say?"

Mimi shook her head.

"That Samantha and Syd are more compatible than we were with them," Jake said.

"Bingo!" Marcel said.

"So what? It's a good thing, no?" Mimi asked.

"Marcel just wants us to be prepared," Jake said.

"Syd should die in love, Jewish or not," Mimi said.

"That makes it easy. Jake?" Marcel said, turning to Jake.

"I keep telling you it's not fucking fair to Samantha."

"She will be adored, cherished, and loved deeply by Syd. In turn, she will love Syd," Marcel said Then he patted Jake's

arm and said, "When the time comes, you will be able to communicate anything and everything you want to Samantha."

"And after? What can you promise after Syd?" Jake asked
in an angry voice.

Marcel flashed a picture of Samantha and felt a deep connection and attraction he longed to pursue. He drew his breath
in, paused, and swiveled his chair around. "If she wants another man after Syd...I will personally...see she's matched ap-
propriately and taken care of."

Jake stood up and asked, "Can I get that in writing?"

"Jake, you sound like a Jewish lawyer," Mimi quipped.

Jake scowled at Mimi and then faced Marcel.

"I've heard stories, Marcel," Jake responded. "I ran into
a few disgruntled group members who said you were getting
sloppy in your matches. That you were doctoring the CM meter to get them out of your hair."

Marcel got defensive. "My track record is clean—just ask
my spirit guides."

Mimi offered, "Marcel, just give him satisfaction or his
money back," and then giggled.

"Easy for you—win-win situation. Syd dies in Samantha's
loving arms and she's left behind with nothing," Jake said

"Consider her spiritual journey," Marcel said, "the brownie points she's banking. She's already up there after dealing
with you. If she attends to Syd, she'll be off the charts in good
karma. Samantha's destined to arrive here a saint—angel of
all angels." Marcel gestured with his arms wide.

"If you put it that way and it's for her development..." Jake
said.

"I can also assure you, when she does get here, you will
have a life together if you both want."

Mimi jumped up and clasped her hands. "Does that mean
Syd and I will also be together when he gets here?"

"That's for him to decide. You fucked with him big time on
Earth. There's no telling what will happen when he finds out
about Damien," Marcel responded.

"I'm more worried about Damien than Syd. What's to become of him?" Mimi asked.

"When you finish your business with Syd, you can attend
to Damien. I warn you, there is not much you can do from
here."

"Why?" Mimi asked.

"He's a troubled soul and will need many lifetimes to learn the harsh lessons," Marcel counseled.

"I don't buy that. There must be something I can do from here," Mimi said.

"Syd's instincts were right. No kids. You forced it and you ended up with a troubled child and, now, a very messed-up adult," Marcel responded.

Mimi didn't accept Marcel's explanation and insisted, "Who are you to judge?"

Marcel turned to her and sternly explained, "You left Syd behind and he raised Damien as his own. He is riddled with guilt for not being able to fix him. Double whammy, in your own words."

Jake piped up, "It just occurred to me: I'm not agreeing to the match if Samantha has to deal with this lunatic Damien."

"*Oy*, more negotiation. Are you sure you're not Jewish?" Mimi asked Jake.

Jake paced the room, getting more exasperated, and asked, "Is that part of the spiritual brownie points? Samantha deals with a dying Syd and his drug-addict son?"

Mimi became indignant and yelled, "My son is not a drug addict. He's just unbalanced."

"*Enough!*" Marcel shouted. "Calm down, both of you! It is what it is. You both know the terms. Do we all agree?"

Jake and Mimi sat down on the sofa, looking at each other. Marcel waved the remote and flashed the image of Syd and Samantha.

"These two people deserve to feel this level of compatibility on Earth. Consider it a gift to them. They may never do better." Marcel bit his lip when he said that. He felt that he would be a perfect match for Samantha and was anxious to get on with the process.

Marcel continued building his case. "You both win here. Mimi gets out of her housedress. Jake, you have unlimited access to Samantha via Syd to tell her what she meant to you. The result is you both move on to a higher level."

Jake responded in a gentler tone, "I want assurance."

Marcel felt he was making progress and decided to throw them a carrot. "I'm going to recommend you both become group mentors. You've been here long enough and know the drill."

Mimi responded, "Frankly, I never want to see this place

again. This viewing room is full of painful memories and GPYF is full of fucking depressing people and stories."

"I agree," said Jake. "Find me a job in the executive cafeteria. I hear those Greek guys hang out talking philosophy. I'm sure Mimi would love working in the sweatshop, designing angel wings and halos."

"Ha! I'm heading back to Earth, asshole," Mimi announced, "and I'm going back as a man!"

Marcel quickly responded, "You have a ways to go, my dear, before they will allow that."

Jake said, "It will be a millennium before they let you back down there!"

As Jake and Mimi continued arguing, Marcel closed his eyes. He meditated out of his body and was drawn to Earth right after Jake's death. Jake's and Mimi's voices trailed off, and he hovered over a storefront, where he saw a downtrodden Samantha sitting in a busy hair salon. She had a large shopping bag at her feet. Marcel entered the body of the male hairdresser, Michel.

Samantha turned to the hairdresser. "Do magic, Michel."

"Honey, you look god-awful. What happened?" Michel/Marcel said. He was exaggerating. Even disheveled, Samantha still looked quite pretty.

"Jake died and he's here in this shopping bag," Samantha said.

Michel/Marcel looked down and saw an urn in the bag. He tried to take it in stride, turning back to study her dull and lifeless hair.

"I hope that was one of his favorite stores," Michel/Marcel remarked.

Samantha smiled weakly as Michel/Marcel ran his fingers through her hair and started massaging her shoulders. He felt electrified but hid it.

Michel/Marcel comforted her, "Courage, babe, you'll get through it. We're going to turn you back into one hot chick."

Samantha looked at herself in the salon mirror and said gloomily, "Do what you can."

As Michel/Marcel released his hands from her shoulders, he was carried back to the viewing room in a jolt, hearing Mimi and Jake arguing loudly and jostling for the remote.

"You say *I* left a mess?" Mimi yelled. "At least I didn't spread a deadly disease to anyone."

Jake responded, "You fucked your shrink— who is probably the father of your child."

Marcel rolled his chair in front of them, faced them, and used his serious low voice.

"This is your last chance, guys. This is the best you will get for your spouses right here and now."

"Is that a threat?" Jake asked.

"A warning. No further spiritual development for either of you if you don't move on and allow this match."

Mimi quickly responded, "I'm all for it. It's him!" She pointed to Jake. "He wants to be in limbo for the next thousand years, banished to the land of lost souls. *Not for me!*"

Marcel moved closer to Jake and took his hands.

"It's in your hands," Marcel said to him. "What's it going to be?"

Jake shook Marcel off and shot up from the sofa but remained silent.

"I can't guarantee any better compatibility now for Samantha. It's going to be intense but brief. I think she's up for it," Marcel said.

"You'll make sure she gets something better after Syd?" Jake asked.

Marcel put his hand on his heart. "I swear on all my spirit guides and the universal almighty, she will have a soft landing."

"Universal almighty? Who the hell is he, or she? You didn't say God, Marcel. I don't hear his name mentioned up here," Mimi said.

"Duh! You just realized? And you've been here how long?" Jake asked.

"Realized what?" Mimi asked back.

"That the atheists are half-right. There is no God. It's a committee—the council, you idiot!" Jake responded.

Mimi gulped and turned to Marcel. "Is that true?"

"I'm afraid so, at least for now. Once there was a God but he's on a sabbatical. He let things get out of control and got tired of all the bullshit politics and bureaucracy up here," Marcel responded.

"Rumor has it they gave him an exit package," Jake reported.

"Not our concern, my children. We have more important matters to consider," Marcel said as he hit the remote, flashing Syd's and Samantha's images with a golden heart-shaped ring around them. "Let's do it!"

Chapter Six

The Heavenly Council

Marcel was conflicted by the decision to match Samantha and Syd. He would finally get rid of Jake and Mimi and send them towards further development. He was also intensely drawn to Samantha. Given Syd's age, it was inevitable Samantha would outlive him, but for how long? What stage and condition would she be in? Maybe she wouldn't want another partner or, worse, be close to leaving the Earth plane herself once Marcel arrived. Would they be a powerful match in his new earthly life?

He needed guidance and requested a joint meeting with his guides and the Heavenly Council. It would kill two birds: clarify his future with Samantha and also negotiate a journey back to Earth, which meant permanently relinquishing his position as GPYF leader. In order to do this, he needed a successor; the only potential one would be Carmella Santini. The loud-mouthed Seaside Psychic came with enormous baggage and needed training, mentoring, and polishing.

Marcel would have to get her husband on Earth matched up and her unruly daughter on track. Otherwise, Carmella would remain distracted and disruptive forever. The last thing the group needed was a leader obsessed with her tits, hair, nails, makeup, and flashy handbags. A strict development plan was required to remove her biases and obsessions while retaining her unbridled enthusiasm and passion. Marcel thought more along the lines of an intervention led by the council, but then he remembered they liked initiatives already in motion.

Marcel decided to consult with his guides first to get advice on how to approach the Heavenly Council. He was determined to be up-front about his conflicting position. Marcel's guides had changed over time and in number but his favorite was the most recent addition. Esmeralda was a "lifer" in Heaven, solely dedicated to spiritual guidance of departed souls and had never had an Earth life. She wore colorful flowing robes, a turban, painted eyebrows, and red lipstick. It was rumored that she was Brazilian bombshell Carmen Miranda's spiritual guide and took on her persona. However, Esmeralda denied such rumors, despite the sounds of a samba preceding her arrival. Her insight and guidance were perfect in tone and content, as was her makeup.

Marcel sent a vibrational message that he needed a consult. Just as he was about to leave the viewing room, he heard the familiar samba music, and in floated Esmeralda—this time with a parrot perched on her shoulder. The air suddenly smelled of tropical fruits.

"Marcel, my darling," Esmeralda's words rolled off her tongue. "You rang?"

The parrot repeated the phrase but she raised her hand to quiet the bird.

"Dear, dear Esmeralda." Marcel quickly approached her and kissed her hand.

"I can feel you are in a dither, my boy," she responded in a caring tone. The parrot repeated "Dither, dither, he's in a dither," at which point Esmeralda rolled her eyes and mentioned that a buffet was being served in the heavenly bird sanctuary. Without hesitation, the parrot flew out of the viewing room, screeching, "Buffet! Buffet!"

"Sorry, he's such a nuisance," she said.

"It's true. I am in a dither," Marcel said, sitting down on the sofa.

Esmeralda sat next to him and took his hand. "You are being pulled down to Earth at lightning speed by love."

Marcel looked into her eyes and asked, "Is it my time? Will I find happiness? Is she the one?"

Esmeralda sat up with shoulders back and announced, "The answers are yes, maybe, probably."

"That's a big help!" Marcel jumped up and paced the room.

Esmeralda asked, "Do you realize why you are drawn to her?"

Marcel said, "She has a name, you know."

"Samantha," Esmeralda corrected herself. "It's because you have a deep connection. You and Samantha are from the same soul tree."

"Do I facilitate the match with this old man? Will I be able to go down and be with her afterward?"

She patted his hand and said, "Until now you have always put your support members' needs ahead of your own. You have dealt with their guilt, bitterness, conflicts, anger, disappointments, and combative behavior. I think the council will see you deserve a break."

Marcel wept as Esmeralda voiced what he had felt for a while.

Esmeralda continued, "The council knows the work you have done: higher rate of success than any match service on Earth. Shit, if you weren't dead, you'd be a billionaire!"

Esmeralda grabbed the remote and flashed in bright lights: "3,987 matches with 2,576 marriages on Earth and Heaven. Sixty-five percent success rate!"

"Many of these matches continue in the spirit world, and the council has taken note," she said.

Marcel respected Esmeralda's opinion and knew he could count on her for advice on how to approach the council. She understood the politics.

"If you ask me, you have all the cards in your hand," she said to Marcel. "You can exit anytime you want."

"I feel obligated to leave the GYPF in good hands. I worked so hard and don't want someone to fuck it up."

"You mean by handing it over to that ditzy Seaside Psychic?" she asked. "Leave her to me for a physical and spiritual makeover."

"We could probably buy her off with an expensive handbag and high heels." Marcel laughed.

"You need to match her uncouth husband and get that brat daughter off her mind. When I get done with her, she'll be a good leader."

Esmeralda was confident that by the time Carmella was ready to take over GPYF, Marcel would be sent back to Earth.

"By then, your Samantha will probably be a widow again and ready for you," Esmeralda said.

Marcel had fears, as there were no guarantees. Esmeralda reminded him that there was no way of knowing how long Samantha and Syd would be together. He knew the rules and the limits of his powers. He couldn't dictate Syd's life expectancy or Samantha's life path, but he could influence them in small ways.

They agreed the first step would be to convince the Heavenly Council to allow Carmella to train as his replacement. The next would be his return to Earth. Esmeralda advised not spelling out his deep longing to be with Samantha. The council was usually made up of hip and tuned-in dudes and gorgeous hermaphrodites. They would read him as if his feelings and desires were tattooed on his forehead.

Marcel was nervous; it had been a while since he had an audience with the Heavenly Council. They might only remember him as Father Mateo.

"You'll have to face them on your own. I've been banned from those meetings as my winged companion here repeats everything they say. When he doesn't like their decisions, he shits on the podium," Esmeralda noted while shaking her head.

She would prep him for the meeting. Training Carmella as his replacement would probably be an easy sell. Despite her eccentricities and obnoxious behavior, Carmella brought people on Earth comfort by transmitting messages from their departed loved ones.

The council might not believe Marcel was ready to return to Earth. They could decide he needed more time on the spirit plane to atone for his reprehensible behavior as Father Mateo. The last thing he wanted was another life review. This time, there might be witnesses, as most of his victims were now probably floating around Heaven.

He knew he was taking chances, to which Esmeralda observed, "You take gambles on Earth, why wouldn't it be the same here?"

She coached him, "You start with your heavenly track record. Don't avoid your past Earth-life indiscretions but address them, and discuss the remediation you took."

Marcel excitedly piped up, "I can point out how I guided my son Luis to the buried treasures and repaid those Indians I ripped off."

Esmeralda continued, "Mention how many degenerate clergy people you have helped to redeem themselves. You are the SME, subject matter expert, up here."

It suddenly crossed Marcel's mind that the council might want him to return to Earth as a religious leader—or worse, as a priest. That would ruin his plan to be with Samantha, unless he ignored his vows and then become another disgraced priest. *Fuck,* he thought. *I would have to start all over again.*

Esmeralda knew what he was thinking. "The last thing you need is another Earth life as a philandering priest gone rogue," she advised.

Marcel agreed. He needed a compelling story about his goals and aspirations for his next incarnation. He and Esmeralda decided he would work on exuding light, happiness, and joy in front of the council. He hoped that alone would be a convincing argument to send him back down. The rumor was that there were plenty of positive people in Heaven and not enough on Earth.

After their session, Esmeralda gave Marcel a kiss on both cheeks. Before she left him, the parrot flew in and perched on her shoulder.

"Good buffet?" she asked him. The parrot cawed loudly as they both faded out of sight. Then Esmeralda's voice suddenly came in loud and clear, "One more thing—they won't let you in dressed like that."

Marcel chuckled, looked down at his jeans, and remembered the dress code.

* * * *

Dressed in a formal white robe, Marcel entered the council chamber, where he hadn't been since he had first proposed his match program. It looked the same: Roman-style spacious chamber with blue tones. It was set up like a US Senate hearing, with a long, slightly curved table so the council members could have eye contact. There were thirteen seats with microphones and buzzers. On the opposite side, there were two tables for cases involving two parties with grievances.

Since this was an individual hearing, Marcel would only occupy one table. He noticed documents and three chairs at the other table. That was disconcerting.

He didn't dare take a seat until the council members had all filed in. There was a drum roll as the back doors opened. Then twelve hip dudes and hermaphrodites, dressed in colorful outfits, entered. The scene resembled a costume party.

They chatted and paid no attention to Marcel. They seated themselves and flipped over their own nameplates on the long table in front of their microphones. The middle seat was empty. He didn't recognize any of them from his last audience.

Marcel deduced that the Heavenly Council must now be a rotating group; otherwise, why would they need nameplates? He thought this was a good sign and no one would remember him as Father Mateo. However, his heart sank when in walked a radiant, bejeweled female figure with upswept blonde hair, dressed in an haute couture gown. She gave him a piercing look. He knew she knew who he was. This would be a tough hearing.

As he sat down, he realized her nameplate was etched in stone while the others were cardboard. It read "Madame." He knew he would be dealing with a power chick, if not *the* power chick.

Madame opened the proceedings and politely welcomed Marcel to the council chamber. She read the rules of the council, dictating they each had only one vote, and she would be the tiebreaker. Marcel had to state his business within five minutes and be prepared for questioning. He or they could call witnesses or provide documentation. Madame reminded Marcel that the council's decision was final and appeals were not permitted. She then gave him the floor.

"Madame and distinguished council members…" Marcel began.

A buzzer went off and Madame frowned at a member, who was dressed as a pirate. He apologized and said it was a mistake, as his eye patch impeded his vision.

Marcel continued, "Some of you may or may not know of the heavenly matchmaking service and support group I have run for a long time."

"I think most of us know who you are, and many of us have been in your group in between Earth lives," Madame responded.

Marcel was relieved and asked, "I hope you were all satisfied with the outcome?"

Several council members chimed in unison, "Yes, yes."

Marcel held his documentation of the matchmaking statistics.

"No reason to prove your track record. Let's cut to the chase, Marcel. Or should I say Father Mateo?" Madame responded curtly. There was a murmur among the members.

"You want to leave us, at least temporarily, and you will match yourself on Earth?" she asked.

Marcel nodded then responded, "Yes, but I want to present plans for my successor and—"

Madame interrupted, "We had a petition from Esmeralda for your replacement and that has been approved. Carmella Santini will be the next GPYF leader. "

Marcel breathed a sigh of relief until he heard her continue, "What we need to agree on *is*—if you are ready for and worthy of returning to Earth."

This was what Marcel was afraid of: a life review and more delays.

"For this purpose, the council will call witnesses," Madame said. "They will weigh in on your fate."

Marcel wondered who the witnesses were. He heard a side door creak open. Two young, Indian-looking men and an elderly woman wearing a shawl entered. They took seats at the table next to Marcel.

He realized who they were—Father Mateo's victims: Luis, Raul, and Natalia. It brought tears to his eyes but he composed himself.

Luis sat in the middle, picked up a document, and read into the microphone.

"Madame and distinguished council members, I, my brother, and mother thank you for this opportunity to address you today and also for a chance to confront this Marcel, whom we knew as Father Mateo."

Luis then stopped reading from the document and turned to face Marcel, who was visibly shaken.

"We forgive him but will never forget. While we recognize he has redeemed himself in many ways up here, he will need to prove himself on Earth," Luis said firmly.

Marcel then feared what was coming next.

"We ask the council to consider our personal agenda and our wish that he be sent down to be matched with Samantha, who has had a hard emotional Earth life; his goal would be to transform that in the best way he knows how."

A flabbergasted Marcel dropped his jaw. He couldn't believe his ears and was perplexed. How did Luis know Samantha? Madame deliberated with the council while they covered their microphones. She then addressed Luis.

"Young man, you present a compelling argument. We thank you for saving the council's time and coming prepared with a statement and a recommendation."

Madame put it to a vote and there were unanimous, "ayes." She pounded a gavel and the session was over.

Marcel tried to catch Luis, Raul, and Natalia's attention but they quickly left the chamber. He was left alone as the costumed council filed out.

Madame was the last to leave. She turned just before exiting, winked at Marcel, and said, "Don't fuck this up."

Chapter Seven

The Launch

Marcel was overjoyed by the council's decision but kept quiet. He gathered the support group together for an announcement.

Jake, Mimi, Carmella, and Bishop wandered into the gazebo. He assured them that the Samantha/Syd match was going forward.

"We're now cleared for takeoff, kids!" Marcel announced.

"I thought it was a done deal?" Jake pointed out.

"Yeah," piped up Mimi, "did you change your mind? Are you double-crossing us?"

"Don't worry. Full speed ahead, but a little matter to resolve," Marcel said.

Carmella suspected something and stared at Marcel. Bishop sat in the corner with an unlit cigarette hanging from his mouth.

"Something's up and Marcel ain't talkin'," Carmella wisecracked.

Bishop took the unlit cigarette out of his mouth and said, "Dude, I'm plumb tired of ya double-talk."

Marcel realized his demeanor caused suspicion and decided to reveal enough to keep them satisfied.

"I will leave my position as support group leader once your partners on Earth are settled. My successor will be one of you but there's a front-runner."

Carmella sat up in her chair and raised her hand. "Me! Me! Pick me!"

Jake interjected, "Do you really think they would make you the group lead? It requires a brain."

"I may not have the brains, but I got *spunk*!" Carmella retorted, then pointed her finger at Jake. "You, Jake Becker,

I know your whole slimy story. Don't forget your Samantha came to me for a reading after you kicked."

Jake responded, "Get out of my face, you blonde bimbo."

Bishop walked over to Jake, raised his fists, and said, "Apologize to the lady...or else."

"Fuck you," Jake yelled and moved away from Bishop. "Marcel, get the show on the road, man."

Bishop walked over to Jake again and looked like he was about to start a fight.

Marcel waved his arms to calm everyone and motioned for them to all sit down. Bishop paid no attention and put his fists out as Jake remained standing, stubborn, and silent. Marcel motioned to Bishop to quit the antics. Bishop gave him the finger and sat down.

Mimi intervened, "Jake, don't jeopardize our deal."

"Don't worry. Marcel won't renege on our deal. He has a personal agenda," said Jake as he sat down.

Marcel confidently said, "I will return to Earth myself, once a suitable incarnation is available."

"I told ya," Jake said.

Carmella, looking at her nails, asked, "Will I be able to get my hair and my nails done if I become the group leader? I should look my best to be a role model."

"Listen up, all of you," Marcel warned. "Once you get your partners settled, you'll all move on. We are about to launch the Syd and Samantha match, but there is some prep."

Carmella raised her hand and asked Marcel, "What are your next steps? So I can learn."

"I need to make their orbits cross naturally. I will keep you posted on their progress," Marcel said as he dismissed the group. The members filed out of the gazebo in silence.

Marcel then sat in his swivel chair in the dark. He held his remote, bit his lip, and flashed an image of Samantha sitting alone, typing on her laptop. Marcel hit the remote, smiled, and said aloud, "Darling Samantha, you are about to get a job you can't refuse."

* * * *

Samantha was unkempt but still attractive at fifty. She wore shorts, a tank top, and her hair in a ponytail. Without makeup, she had a glow about her. She wore stylish reading glasses as she sat in her home office, reading emails. Suddenly, the computer beeped, announcing the arrival of a new email. She opened it up and started reading.

Her lanky high school senior son popped his head into her office and asked, "When are we eating, Mom?"

Samantha glanced at the clock and then the setting sun outside their Delray Beach, Florida, condo and replied, "Why don't you order a pizza, hon? I've got to answer this email."

Samantha grabbed her handbag and rummaged through it, looking for her wallet. She took out a twenty and handed it to Bobby. He made a face.

"I forgot; you're still growing and need lots of nutritious pizza. Get two," Samantha said as she pulled out another twenty and handed it to him. She quickly returned to her screen.

"What's so important?" Bobby asked. "Is it a job?"

"Maybe," Samantha said casually.

"Good. I'm tired of being poor," Bobby commented.

"We were never poor. I just didn't want to eat into our capital, hon."

"Living on ramen is no fun," Bobby said.

"You want the fifty-five-thousand-dollar-a-year college. So it's ramen three days a week. Jake left us dead broke, pun intended. Look how lucky we are: a condo, college, and two cars."

Bobby smirked. Samantha noted, "Not to mention I could have been dead from AIDS by now."

"Oh yeah, I forgot," Bobby said as the phone rang. He picked it up.

"Mister Becker? That's my dad. He's not here right now; he's being held at Guantanamo."

Samantha grabbed the phone and clicked it off. "Bobby!" She sighed, making a face.

"They were selling life insurance. Ha! That would've been funny. No sale, suckers; he's already dead," Bobby said with a giggle.

"Order the goddamn pizzas and let me answer this email. Hey, it's a job in New York City. Two hours from your college," Samantha said with a twinkle in her eye.

"I'm thrilled, Mummy! *Not,*" Bobby said in a fake British accent as he spun around and exited Samantha's office.

Samantha didn't allow herself to get excited. She had too

many disappointing job interviews in the past year. She would go with the flow but this job did sound different. It was perfect for her. Samantha had a twenty-year track record in managing overseas call centers. Mercury Partners, a major consulting firm, had an opening for a vice president of operations, based in New York but with heavy overseas travel.

Each time she fantasized about the job in New York, she stopped herself. It had been thirty years since she lived there. It was long before Jake. What would it be like to be back in Manhattan? Theaters, concerts, and restaurants. Would she finally meet someone? She reread the job description several times and finally sent her resume to the headhunter who had contacted her.

Samantha felt she had a good shot at the New York job. She didn't want to think about the implications of moving. Somehow it would be easier, packing Bobby up for college while she moved to take a job in the same state. She saw a change coming; not only as an empty nester but as a participant in something dramatic, life transforming.

Bobby had announced that there would be no more men around until after he left home. He was given a raw deal with men in his life and gave up on potential father figures. There was his dead bio dad, Jake, and then Alfonso—the abusive bipolar Argentinean boyfriend.

Bobby devoured an entire large pizza on his own. Samantha managed to grab one slice and returned to her laptop. She reread the email from the headhunter, Lyle Hackett. He was vague about how he had found her. She Googled him and found his LinkedIn profile. He looked very attractive, had an impressive background, and was probably about her age.

As she searched for more information, the phone rang. It was Lyle. He had a very sexy voice. He apologized for calling her at dinner time but said he was impressed with her resume. He said he usually met with candidates before asking for a resume, but she was referred by a reliable source. *Who is this "reliable source,"* Samantha wondered.

Lyle wanted to meet with her at his Florida office the next afternoon. The more Lyle spoke and effervesced with compliments about her background, the more excited Samantha became. *Fuck the job,* Samantha thought. *I just want to meet Lyle!*

* * * *

Marcel smiled, clicked off the image of the attractive Samantha busy at her laptop, and sighed deeply. He was going down to embody Lyle Hackett. He sat, fantasizing about being in Samantha's presence, when Jake and Mimi entered the gazebo. They wanted to know what progress Marcel had made on the match.

"Impatient, are we?" Marcel said. "You two were at each other's throats over this match and now you can't wait."

"Just want to make sure you're going through with it," Jake said.

"There's a lot of planning. You can't just force these two people together like that," Marcel said, snapping his fingers.

Mimi piped up, "So what's with all the complications already? Just get them together and that off-the-charts chemistry should do the rest."

"Do you think having them meet at the supermarket deli counter or at Starbucks is going to work?" Marcel asked in an aggravated tone.

"What's a Starbucks?" Mimi asked.

Jake shook his head. "Just show us you're making progress. No need to get testy," Jake replied.

Marcel sat down, grabbed the remote, and flashed diagrams and a timeline. At this point, he was improvising as he hadn't yet planned out the entire timeline. He was so excited about his forthcoming journey down to Earth as Lyle Hackett that he hadn't yet planned the next steps. So he wrote as he flashed the boxes, "Step one: Samantha, in Florida, gets a call from a local headhunter about a job opportunity in New York."

He flashed another box and wrote, "Syd, New York."

"Step two: Samantha is intrigued by this job, which pays well and is perfect for her. Also..." Marcel flashes another box, "Bobby Becker will attend college within driving distance from New York City, yet another incentive to take the job."

Mimi asked, "Is she going to hit my Syd up for the tuition?"

"Shut up, Mimi. You want this match or not?" Jake yelled. "What's not covered by scholarship, Samantha is covering with insurance money she invested when I died...*so there!*"

"Let's move on," said Marcel as he wrote. "Step three: Samantha goes on an interview in New York."

"Is that when they meet?" Mimi asked excitedly.

"Premature," Marcel said. "These two will need common ground and coincidences that make them pay attention. Step four: Samantha returns to Florida and gets a phone call—"

Mimi interrupted, "From Syd?"

"No, from Jerry Feingold." Marcel illuminated a box of the diagram.

"Who the fuck is that?" Jake asked.

"Samantha's cousin Barbara's attorney in New York, who is also Syd's friend."

"Don't know the guy. Probably friends after I died," Mimi said.

"Barbara? She was a recovering drug addict when I was alive," Jake noted.

"Jerry Feingold helped expunge her drug arrests," Marcel responded.

Marcel had many boxes on the diagram with lines drawn in between.

"There were other possible connections," Marcel said as he flashed several other connections, "but this one is a fast track."

Marcel described how Syd told Jerry Feingold that he wanted to spend the winter in Florida. Did he know some nice, maybe non-Jewish women? Jerry said he had a client, Barbara, whose cousin, Samantha, was definitely a *shiksa* and maybe could help him network.

"Step five: Jerry gives Syd Samantha's photo and telephone number. Step six: Samantha gets the job in New York. The company's offices are a few blocks from Syd's apartment."

"This sounds very complex and fraught with potential holes," Jake said.

"Trust me," Marcel said, looking into Jake's eyes. "I'll drive every step and I will course correct if needed."

"I hope you know what you're doing," Mimi said. "Our future here depends on it. I need to get out of this housedress!"

Marcel stood up, ushered Jake and Mimi to the doorway, and said, "I need to be alone to oversee Samantha's meeting with the headhunter."

He failed to mention he would be Lyle Hackett.

Chapter Eight

Samantha and Marcel

Samantha could hardly sleep, thinking about Lyle Hackett. She felt a strong connection over the phone and was entranced by his profile photo. She tried forcing herself to think that her attraction was misguided and a result of not having been on a date for three years.

The fact was, not many men interested her. When they did, they always said or did something to ruin any slight attraction she might feel. Then there was the looming issue of her HIV status. She was terrified of being rejected and avoided men for that reason.

In her fantasy about Lyle, she imagined he would take her HIV status in stride. She didn't have any issues with her ex-boyfriend. Alfonso thought it was a ploy to avoid having sex on their first date. When she flashed Jake's death certificate and pointed to the cause of death, he still didn't believe her. Alfonso would just grab her ass and say, "Nothing wrong with this hot babe."

Just in case Lyle was as attractive as his photo and available, she would prep accordingly. Samantha looked in the mirror and decided she needed professional help. She made an appointment with her hairdresser and another with a makeup artist. To save time, she did her own nails and shaved her legs instead of waxing at the salon, as she intended going barelegged. He might be a leg man so catching sight of stubbly leg hair could ruin the deal. She rummaged through her closet, looking for a suit that fit. She settled on black as it would make her look thinner.

She planned on running to Lyle's office from the hair salon so she would look freshly coiffed and made-up. Then she had doubts. He was probably unavailable.

She panicked at the possibility of him being short. At just over five foot nine, Samantha needed a tall man next to her. In high heels, she was over six feet. With all this beautification prep, she temporarily forgot the real reason for meeting Lyle.

While her hair was being blow-dried, ironed, and lacquered, she looked up the latest info on the hiring company and took mental notes. She wanted to appear well-informed and interested in the job. So, if Lyle turned out to be a bust, then maybe the job in New York was a real opportunity.

* * * *

Marcel, now embodied in Lyle, was equally nervous and concerned that he looked too formal for his meeting with Samantha. He looked in his private executive-bathroom mirror and saw a wavy light-brown-haired, blue-eyed, well-groomed middle-aged man in an expensive suit and tie. He took the tie off; he didn't want to look intimidating. Maybe business casual was better. Then he noticed gray at the temples but decided it made him look more distinguished.

He was anxious to have private face time with Samantha and an excuse to have her talk about herself. Marcel/Lyle forgot the real purpose of the meeting and was absorbed in the anticipation of being in Samantha's aura.

Samantha arrived ten minutes before their meeting time so as not to appear too eager. She shook with anticipation. When the receptionist, Katy, wasn't looking, she practiced deep breathing.

Marcel/Lyle sprayed himself with expensive cologne just as he heard that Samantha arrived. He decided to put the tie back on and meet her in the boardroom.

Samantha was shown in by Katy, who instructed her to sit at a long mahogany table. It was a dimly lit, tastefully furnished boardroom with expensive artwork. She was happy it was not lit by bright fluorescent lights in case her makeup was too heavy for daytime. She continued the deep breathing as the double doors opened and in walked Marcel/Lyle. She stood up, extended her hand, and introduced herself.

"Hi, I'm Samantha Becker," she said in a breathy voice.

Lyle/Marcel was overcome with excitement and almost tripped over a chair.

"So, *so* pleased to meet you, Samantha. Lyle Hackett."

He shook her hand a little longer than usual for a business setting. Samantha thought she felt a little squeeze but wasn't sure.

He stood five nine or ten, so her fears about him being a shrimp were alleviated. She felt his warmth and then noticed him gazing at her. She searched for a ring but his fingers were bare.

Marcel/Lyle was vindicated and his attraction to Samantha was real. Those images in the viewing room didn't betray him. He knew she could also felt it.

Samantha reiterated her interest in the job. She smiled a lot and studied his hair, his suit, and his demeanor. He reviewed her resume that was already on the table and asked about her past experience. When it came to the gap in employment, Samantha explained being a caregiver for her sick husband who had died. She wanted to make it clear she was single.

Marcel/Lyle imagined what Jake would say if he were here in the room with his wife, seeing Samantha flirting with him and being unemotional about his death. It was clear Samantha had moved on and was ready for a new and serious love.

Marcel/Lyle scanned her resume. "Active in the Boy Scouts?" he asked.

"My son's troop. Merit badge counselor for all the 'sissy' badges like music, drama, and art," Samantha responded playfully.

Lyle laughed and then continued to a more serious subject.

"I see several nonprofit boards including one serving children with HIV." He was curious to see if this made her emotional, but she was stoic. He wanted so much to take her in his arms and tell her how he knew about her suffering and the details of Jake's death. As he reached over and was about to pat Samantha's hand, he suddenly heard the sounds of a samba and then the caw of a parrot; he withdrew. He knew Esmeralda was observing this meeting. Then her booming voice came through to him alone, "I told you not to fuck this up."

"He's fucking it up, fucking it up," her parrot said.

Esmeralda demanded, "What the hell are you doing, Marcel? Stay on task. You're setting her up for this job, not for falling into your arms. Stop thinking with your dick."

Marcel/Lyle was jolted back into the room while Samantha talked about her last job.

Then Katy knocked and entered the room, wearing her headset and attached microphone. "Mister Hackett, your wife's on line two. She says it's urgent." He knew Esmeralda orchestrated that interruption to force him back into reality.

Marcel/Lyle slipped and said, "Thanks, Esmeralda."

Katy left the boardroom and Samantha said, "I thought her name was Katy?"

"Umm, Esmeralda is our regular gal. Katy's just a temp," Lyle/Marcel shot back.

Then it hit her: Lyle was fucking married!

He excused himself, got up, and lifted a phone on the side table. He put the receiver to his ear for a second and then hung up. "Hello... Hello... No one there." He returned to the table and considered telling Samantha he wasn't really married. He knew Esmeralda was right—he was off script and needed to facilitate a Samantha and Syd match, not pursue his own agenda.

Samantha tried to hide her disappointment and steered the conversation to the job opening. Marcel/Lyle changed his tone and confirmed that his client was interested in interviewing her.

"When are you available to go to New York?" he asked. He felt her mood shift and longed for her to validate her feelings for him. Marcel/Lyle had to let it go because it was not their time.

"I could travel as early as next week," Samantha piped up. She shifted gears and forced herself to find Lyle Hackett unappealing due to being unavailable. She also imagined he was a cheater and a shitty husband.

"You've got a good shot at this job," Marcel/Lyle responded.

Samantha now thought of his agenda as receiving a placement commission should she get the job. He'd do anything at this point. They shook hands. She left the office, feeling foolish for thinking this guy was a potential man in her life. What she didn't know was that, as she left the boardroom, Marcel/Lyle caught sight of her shapely, smooth legs and immediately got a hard-on.

Back in her condo, she looked in the bathroom mirror at her freshly coiffed hair and fading makeup; then started to cry. When she heard Bobby come in, she quickly dabbed her eyes and composed herself.

"How did it go? Did you get the job?" Bobby yelled from the kitchen while poking his head in the fridge.

"It was just the headhunter. The job interview is next week in New York," Samantha responded.

"Good. What's for dinner?" Bobby asked in a loud voice.

Samantha groaned and shouted back, "Why don't you cook for a change!" She heard the fridge door slam shut.

Samantha did love Bobby unconditionally. She felt strongly he was the reason she survived the past fifteen years after losing Jake.

Those first years were rough, digging out of the debt Jake left. Then she worried about HIV and dying of AIDS before Bobby was in kindergarten. With courage and determination, she soldiered through, getting a job, an MBA, and a house and starting a college fund for Bobby. She vowed to get out of debt and make enough money to provide for him should she die young.

Samantha was afraid of discrimination, so she stayed in the closet about Jake's illness. To anyone who asked, Jake died of leukemia. She told Bobby the truth when he was fifteen and he took it in stride, including the fact that she was infected.

He even made a bad joke once when she cut herself. As he helped put pressure on the wound, he said, "Going to wash my hands so I don't get AIDS." It was a big relief for Samantha that Bobby had no evidence of the killer virus when he was finally tested.

She was proud that she saved enough to allow Bobby to follow his dream of studying film. Even when he was away at college, she knew they would always remain close; after all, she was his only parent. She feared that someday he would marry a cold-hearted bitch, who would fleece her and shut her up in a nursing home.

She often suggested to Bobby, "You should marry an Asian girl or a Latina for my sake. They respect old people."

He would make a sour face and joke, "What makes you think I'm marrying a girl?"

"It's *okay* if you're gay. The Asian guys and Latinos also treat their mothers gently."

Bobby then patted her hand and assured her, "Don't worry, Mom; I'll put you somewhere nice."

As Samantha put her hair in a ponytail, Bobby sensed she felt low. He took the initiative to heat up leftovers. At the table, she poured herself a glass of wine and tried to stop beating herself up over Lyle Hackett.

They ate in silence until Bobby piped up, "Barbara left you a message, about her attorney and an email she sent."

Samantha thought that it sounded strange but shrugged it off.

"Probably wants me as a character witness in court again," Samantha said.

Her cousin had a history of getting in legal jams and filing restraining orders on her many boyfriends. Jerry Feingold was a four-times-married, elderly playboy attorney who felt sorry for Barbara and her checkered past. He didn't charge her very much for his legal services. Recently, he helped her sue a supermarket where she fell and broke her ankle.

Samantha often wondered if Barbara was having sex with him, especially when he was in between marriages.

After dinner, Bobby planted himself in front of the TV while Samantha went to her laptop. With her second glass of wine in hand, she read her emails. Barbara's email was red with an urgent flag attached.

> Hi Cousin Sam,
>
> Hope all is well. I'm FABULOUS! Just got a settlement from the supermarket lawsuit. Jerry did a FABULOUS job. Of course he gets a cut, A BIG CUT! Greedy SOB, well, he is a Jewish lawyer. LOL. Speaking of Jerry, he has a friend called Syd who's going to Florida for the winter and wants to know if you would go out to dinner with him. He may be a little old for you, babe, but HEY, FREE FOOD! Jerry's been such a doll. DO ME A BIG FAVOR, WILL YA, CUZ?
>
> IT'S TIME FOR YOU TO GET OUT OF YOUR SOCIAL RUT!
>
> You're still "one hot babe," always have been.
>
> LUV BABS

The "hot babe" comment was from one of Barbara's greaser boyfriends, made about Samantha years ago.

Samantha reread Barbara's email, then answered. She would go out with this Syd. She signed it, "*From Sam, the still-hot babe.*"

The next morning, Barbara forwarded an email from Jerry with Syd's photo and phone number. She glanced at it and went about her business. Samantha was psyching herself up for New York. *It is not the time to meet a man,* she thought, as she buried the Lyle Hackett incident and any hope of romance.

* * * *

Back in the viewing room, Marcel sat in his swivel chair and replayed their boardroom meeting. Marcel freeze-framed Samantha's expressions of excitement when they first met. He wondered what would've happened if he made a play for her. Lyle Hackett was a temporary gig and he knew it. He put his head in his hands, realizing that Samantha was now in Syd's orbit. It was only a matter of time before they would meet and experience the powerful chemistry.

He promised himself he wouldn't be jealous or upset. As much as it pained him to watch her with another man, he had an obligation to Jake and Mimi. He facilitated Samantha's destiny and she needed the elderly Syd to awaken her. Marcel had no choice but to go with the flow. He had to be patient and, when the time came, he would be with her on Earth in body and soul.

Chapter Nine

Good Phone

Syd hadn't seen his attorney friend, Jerry Feingold, since his fourth wife left him for a young stud. They sat in a New Jersey diner and flirted with the harried, middle-aged, blonde waitress, who humored them because she was after a decent tip from the two geezers. Jerry, a short, stocky, silver-haired fox in his sixties, was dressed in a navy blazer with an open-collar shirt and reeked of after shave. He sat across from six-foot-two Syd, a bald, slender, and distinguished-looking seventy-year-old, who wore a suit and one of his infamous ties.

"Syd, what the hell is on your tie? Women's legs?" Jerry giggled. He found Syd's ties kitschy, but his charm and charisma made up for it.

"I see you're still getting manicures," Syd remarked, looking at Jerry's nails.

"Great way to meet women," Jerry responded. "Those Korean girls are great matchmakers. Met my third wife in a nail salon."

"Don't they make people think you're gay?" Syd asked.

"Well-groomed. You should try it," Jerry said, shaking a packet of sugar. He noticed his cup was empty and called over to the waitress, "Could I get more coffee, hon. Make sure it's fresh."

"Tell me about your client," Syd said, changing the subject.

"Barbara! She's a trip," Jerry responded.

"She's not Jewish; that's what counts," Syd said.

"I hear ya. You want a woman who makes dinner and not reservations."

"Is this Barbara intelligent, good-looking, and tall?" Syd asked.

"Whoa, I'm not setting you up with Barbara," Jerry

clarified. "Most of Barbara's guys are tattooed, missing teeth, have permanent broken noses, and wear ankle monitors."

"Then why did you leave a message about her?" Syd asked.

"We're setting you up with her cousin, who lives in Delray Beach. Sounds like you have a lot in common," Jerry said, sipping his coffee. Then he noted, "Sam's a lot younger than you, but hey, you never know. I sent you an email this morning with the LinkedIn profile and telephone number."

"Sam? Do I look like a *fegalah*?" Syd asked in a concerned voice.

"Short for Samantha, nitwit. You, gay? Never." Jerry laughed. Then he changed the subject to what Syd really had on his mind besides women: his will and power of attorney.

"I'm leaving everything to Damien and cutting Alana out completely," Syd responded.

Jerry patted Syd's hand and said, "Good move. I never understood why you included her. She doesn't deserve it."

"I felt bad when Murray and Fran threw Alana out of the house. She didn't commit a crime; she's just a lesbo," Syd remarked. "I'm giving her a last hand-out and telling her so."

Syd's niece was an emotional and financial burden that he couldn't seem to control. As a child, she was always close to Syd—hugging and kissing him when he visited. She was the daughter he would never have. Syd felt obligated to her, ever since she came out of the closet and Murray and Fran rejected her. They also swindled her out of her inheritance from her grandmother. Now, Alana was an unstable, middle-aged, lesbian hypochondriac. She couldn't keep a job and tended to pair up with similarly unstable lesbian partners, who were usually obese and unhealthy.

Besides giving hand-outs to Alana, Syd sometimes ended up helping her partners as well. Once Alana's wheelchair-bound girlfriend needed three grand for a root canal and Syd caved.

As much as Syd cared about Alana, she and her lesbian girlfriends were an affront to his keen sense of style and beauty. He suggested Alana use his hand-outs for a makeover and a new wardrobe. He often wondered why she couldn't be a lipstick lesbian in heels.

When Alana was homeless and jobless at twenty-six, Syd invited her to live temporarily with him and Damien. He thought Damien might benefit from having a 'big sister'. Syd had to throw Alana out of the house when he caught her selling her antidepressants to a twelve-year-old Damien.

Jerry sipped his coffee and asked, "Who do you want as power of attorney in case you're incapacitated? Executor? Pull your life support?"

Syd took a deep breath and said quietly, "Not Damien; he'd probably jump the gun for the few dollars I have left. Need to think that one over."

"Understand. I don't trust my kids either or any of my wives. They'd fight over who would get the privilege to pull my plug," Jerry joked.

Then Jerry changed to a serious tone of voice. "Syd, this is important. If you don't trust Damien, who else is there?"

Syd didn't respond but knew Jerry had a point; he had no one else. Damien was his only son and he felt responsible for his battle with drugs and alcohol. He paraded him to a myriad of doctors when he was a child and nothing helped. Syd remembered Mimi's shrink, Dr. Stern, had no luck either. Whatever happened to that guy?

He let one psychiatrist talk him into sending Damien to a 'therapeutic' boarding school in Maine for disturbed teens. He ran away several times and eventually ended up at sixteen in a juvi detention center for stealing a car. Syd hoped that someday Damien would straighten out; but at age forty, that possibility was getting more remote every day. Syd's coping mechanism was to 'compartmentalize', which really meant denial in anyone else's book.

As they left the diner, Jerry gave Syd a heartfelt hug and told him to let him know his decision; he would draw up the documents. He also reminded him to check his email and call Barbara's cousin. "You never know," he said with a twinkle in his eye.

Syd returned to his two-bedroom co-op apartment in the Murray Hill section of Manhattan, in a building called The Colony. He finished the *New York Times* and then went online to find information about this Samantha. Wouldn't it be great to date a younger woman in Florida for the winter, preferably a serious, intelligent woman? He was done with the shenanigans and games of his last girlfriends.

He checked Jerry's email with Samantha's contact information. He went to her LinkedIn profile. Her photo looked like she had light brown, almost blonde, hair and sparkling eyes.

She is pretty, he thought, and looked younger than her fifty years, but maybe it was an old photo. Also, it was just a head shot. What if she were obese, or just chubby? He couldn't deal with that. However, her academic credentials and work experience were impressive, with several decades at major corporations. He hoped it wasn't all bullshit.

Then he realized they both attended New York University, although fifteen years apart. He also noticed her high school was a mile from the door factory he owned back in the 1970's and '80s. That was odd.

Syd, not being shy, decided to call Samantha but got her voicemail. He left a message identifying himself as a friend of Jerry Feingold. He went back to his laptop and fantasized about Samantha. He imagined them together, what she might smell like, or what her lips would feel like. This gave him a rush and a small hard-on, as much as could be expected for a seventy-year-old with prostate troubles.

* * * *

Samantha wasn't in Florida when Syd left his message. She was in Manhattan only blocks away from Syd's apartment, having her final job interview. She thought the interview had gone well but prepared herself for the worst. She felt energized, being on the streets of Manhattan again; it reminded her of her college days. Her cell phone rang as she packed her bags in preparation for returning to Florida.

Marcel/Lyle allowed himself a last contact with Samantha. "How did the interview go?" he asked.

Samantha was lukewarm with Lyle and said modestly, "I think it went well." She thanked him for the opportunity. Talking to him reminded her of her misguided feelings.

Though Lyle/Marcel knew she would get the job, he went through the motions. He said he would reach out to his client and find out if she was a final candidate. He sounded extra friendly on the phone and asked personal questions.

Samantha made an excuse that she was checking out of the hotel and had to get off the phone. She felt uneasy about Lyle.

When Samantha didn't return Syd's phone call by the next morning, he pondered whether to call her again but decided against it. He asked his elderly neighbor, who advised him to give it another day.

Judy was one of several women in Syd's apartment building that checked in on him regularly and brought him casseroles in the evening. If there was no food at the door or a dinner invitation, he would go out, mostly alone. He felt desolate and was so ready for a new love in his life, he could taste it.

* * * *

Samantha arrived at her Delray Beach condo to the sound of a video game blasting. Bobby was playing with gamers in another time zone. Samantha heard him cursing and tapped on the door to let him know she was home.

She found him with the controller in his hands, standing, and screaming at the screen, "Come on, assholes; clear that beach! We're going to lose!"

Bobby quickly turned around, covered the microphone attached to his headset, and said, "Hi, how did it go? Did you get it?" He returned to watch the screen, and then quickly put his headset back on and continued screaming, "Hey, get those bastards!"

Samantha gave up trying to have a conversation with him and went to the kitchen. She saw a light flashing on the phone. She listened to her voice mails. There was one from the day before, a man who introduced himself as "Syd Weis, a friend of Jerry Feingold. Can you call me back at your convenience?" and gave his phone number.

At first, she was confused but then remembered Barbara's email. She reread the email that said he was sixty-five and sold doors and windows. She Googled him and found references to his business, awards from five years ago, and then a reference to a Rockaway Beach High School reunion that put him at seventy and not sixty-five. So, he had one strike against him. She thought she would call Syd back as a courtesy to Jerry, who helped Barbara for so many years. Syd answered right away, as though he waited with the phone at his side.

"Hi, this is Samantha Becker; Barbara's cousin?"

"Ah yes, Samantha. Thank you for calling me back."

Syd was enthralled by Samantha's voice. He immediately thought *sexy.*

"Sorry I didn't get back to you yesterday, but I just returned from Manhattan, where I was on a job interview."

"Were you really? What a shame. I would've liked to invite you out for lunch or dinner."

Samantha thought that was very aggressive.

"Probably would've been nice to have had a drink before the interview to calm me down," she joked. "Then again, as it was ten a.m., probably not a good idea."

"I'm sure you're a confident woman who can hold her own," Syd said, gushing with enthusiasm.

"I'm glad it's over," Samantha said.

Samantha was surprised he knew a lot about the company she interviewed with. He appreciated her qualifications and expertise for the job. He got points for that. So far, he had said nothing to turn her off.

Syd was anxious to grill her on her love life. What if she were seeing someone? Was she online looking for men? More importantly, was she fat?

Samantha brought up the subject of children, which opened the door to discussion about spouses. Syd told her about having a son and then the tragic death of his wife. Samantha was taken aback to learn Syd was left a widower in his thirties with a young child, just as she was left a widow with young Bobby. She told him about Jake and her experience as a single parent.

"Have you had any relationships since?" Syd asked coyly.

"One relationship with a bipolar Latino," Samantha responded, "which ended with a restraining order."

Syd breathed a sigh of relief; no competition. Then he posed an important question.

"Have you ever dated older men? You know, I'm about fifteen years your senior."

"Twenty, to be exact; the Internet is full of info."

"I see," Syd said.

Samantha sighed and nonchalantly told Syd about her affair with a man twenty-five years her senior when she was twenty. "Older men don't scare me; assholes do."

Syd laughed and said, "You do good phone."

Samantha thought that sounded pornographic and laughed. Their conversation flowed and there was an immediate high comfort level. Syd asked if he could call her again and when.

Samantha was confused, as she thought he would be coming to Florida at some point and take her out to dinner. Since when did this become a hookup? She was bemused by Syd and decided to go with the flow.

After their initial conversation, they both went back online to examine each other's photos. The problem was the photo attached to Barbara's email came with that of another old man, so she wasn't sure which one was Syd and which was Jerry.

Did it really matter? She was curious and emailed Barbara to find out. Was it the guy on the right or left? She hoped it was the right.

Syd showed Samantha's photo to Judy and asked her advice. Judy was encouraging and told him to go for it.

"What do you have to lose? You're not getting any younger, *bubbelah*," Judy remarked. "If she's looking for a multimillionaire, tell her to look elsewhere."

Judy reminded Syd of his mother but Judy could be a moaner. She complained daily about her children and grandchildren not visiting. She also talked incessantly about her aches and pains and was a pill popper.

Syd didn't call Samantha for three days. She was surprised that she cared about this. She figured he was just another flake and forgot about it.

On the fourth day, he phoned. They spoke about movies and music. Samantha took a risk and told Syd about her brief career as a lounge singer. He was thrilled and begged her to send him a recording.

While they were still on the phone, Samantha emailed Syd several MP3 files of old recordings she had made with a jazz trio. He downloaded the files while they were still talking and she could hear him listening to her singing Cole Porter's "*Let's Do It, Let's Fall in Love,*" which became his favorite. Syd was enthralled and played it over and over again. He called Judy over to listen.

"The girl's got talent," Judy remarked. "She should go on *American Idol* already."

Syd played it for everyone who came by, including the black doorman, who came up to deliver a package, and then for the housecleaner. Syd took the song as an invitation to fall in love with Samantha.

What Samantha didn't mention was that it was also Jake's favorite recording, which he liked to listen to often—even on the day he died.

The coincidences were getting scary and Samantha wanted validation before she continued having "good phone" with Syd. She decided to ask Barbara to do a recon mission: meet Syd in person and report back.

Samantha didn't want to waste any more good phone time if he was an idiot in person.

Chapter Ten

New Group Leader in Training

Carmella, in a sequined gold lamé jacket, palazzo pants, and chunky high heels, sat in Marcel's chair and held the remote. Marcel looked on, giving commands.

"This is so hard. You make it look so easy," Carmella said. She fiddled with the controller and only produced scrambled images. "I'll never do it," she moaned.

"Relax. You have to concentrate," Marcel said.

"I want to see what my Frankie is up to," she said. "Better not be up to no good."

"You have to let go and move on; he has." Marcel grabbed the controller and produced an image of Frank dancing with a buxom blonde, who looked remarkably like Carmella.

"Look, she could be your twin sister," Marcel remarked.

"Holy Christ! Oops, sorry, Bob," she said, looking around embarrassed. "Hope he didn't hear that."

"Detach or this won't work out."

"I guess I should be flattered he picked a broad who looks like me. Who the fuck is she?"

"Does it matter? Frank looks happy," Marcel said.

Carmella shot up from the chair and put her fingers through her short blonde hair with dark roots.

Marcel interjected, "He may not need a new partner just now. You've got work to do if you want to take over my job."

Carmella sat down and calmly asked, "Where the hell, I mean where the heaven are you going?"

"Not sure," Marcel said coyly.

"Let me guess. When the shit hits the fan in this Samantha and Syd business, you're the knight in shining armor. Am I right?"

Marcel didn't respond.

"Busted!" Carmella said and continued, "You forget, I read the dead from down there. Haven't lost my touch; I can read you too, sometimes."

Marcel shifted uncomfortably in his chair. "I guess this is why you are so suitable for this job."

"So, spill."

"It's not a given that I'm returning to Earth. If you can't take this over, there's no one else around."

"You can't tell me with all the goddamn dead people up here, there's no other qualified person except for me?"

"Maybe you were chosen."

"By who?"

"By whom," Marcel corrected.

"You see, I can't talk English. Why would you want me in charge?"

"You have the potential to evolve. Your abilities were extraordinary on Earth and you could be very powerful up here."

"Really?" Carmella asked proudly.

"The spirits you connected with are in the thousands, as are the people on Earth to whom you brought comfort. I certainly didn't come with any of those qualifications. In fact, I did a lot of damage during my last Earth life."

"Yes, I heard—naughty, naughty priest," Carmella said.

"I have powerful guides here and I am passing them on to you." He summoned Esmeralda.

The sounds of a samba filled the gazebo. Carmella looked around, puzzled.

"It's Esmeralda, and she will take over your training," Marcel said.

Esmeralda floated in, wearing her usual colorful outfit. The smell of fruit wafted behind her.

"Carmella, my dear. You're going for a makeover, but it won't be what you expect. It's my way or the highway, darling."

Carmella jumped up and negotiated with Esmeralda. "I really want to stay a blonde. My natural hair color is so blah. I won't look good in long hair unless I get a chin implant, and then maybe. What about a brow lift? Boob job...I had such great ones before the mastectomy. Surely there's got to be great reconstruction guys up here. Tummy tuck wouldn't be bad either. They serve a lot of carbs up here. Look, I'm forced to wear an elastic waistband; see? My skin is still good; never reached menopause...still full of estrogen, thank God. Oh, sorry; forgot, he's history."

"We do have our work cut out for us," Esmeralda said as she and Carmella left the gazebo.

* * * *

Jake, Mimi, and Bishop entered the gazebo.

"I have news. Bishop is returning to Earth," Marcel announced.

"Don't know if I should be thrilled or not. Hope it's not someone's pet hamster," Bishop remarked.

"You're going back as a human to make it right with Velma and your kid. It was sanctioned by the council. You still love her, don't you?" Marcel asked.

"Well, of course I do! Does the sun rise every morning… at least on Earth? I thought about it. I feel bad about her being forced into the arms of that fathead robber," Bishop responded.

"There's one twist. You have to go back as a woman," Marcel said.

"What?" Bishop said, alarmed.

"Velma switched teams after your buddy Fathead died. The best way to make her life complete would be to return as a woman," Marcel said.

"Velma, a goddamned rug muncher? No way," Bishop yelled.

"We could match her up, but I thought you would want the chance," Marcel mentioned.

Bishop looked puzzled and concerned, then asked, "But as a girl? My kid's gonna have two mommies?"

"You can go down and be a mommy to your kid, or we can arrange a match with another woman," Marcel said. "Let's see, there are a couple of lesbian connections right here in this room. Jake's daughter and maybe Syd's niece?"

Jake made the sign of the cross with two fingers and said to Marcel, "What? My daughter is gay and you want to match her up with white trash?"

"Double whammy," Mimi said, laughing. "Must be hereditary."

"Well, shut my mouth." Bishop plopped onto the sofa, shaking his head, and didn't hear what Jake said. "My only choice? Find a woman for Velma or return to Earth as a chick?"

Jake piped up, "How come he gets to go back and I can't? I petitioned several times and got turned down."

"You have more work to do up here," Marcel responded.

"Isn't it three strikes and you're out?" Jake asked.

Bishop responded, "Don't feel so bad. Would you want to go back as a dyke?"

Jake continued, "I'd go back as the hunchback of Notre Dame to prevent Samantha from being thrown into the hands of that old man."

"Too late," Mimi said. "Right, Marcel?"

"It's in motion. They have met telephonically," Marcel responded.

"Not too late. When he dies, and he will, I can be there to pick up the pieces," Jake said.

Marcel said, "That may not be part of her destiny path. The Heavenly Council has another agenda for Samantha, once Syd crosses over."

"I don't care. I'll change their minds. I think I have a compelling argument," Jake said.

Mimi piped up, "Leave it alone. Syd and Samantha are going to be together. Just accept it already. I spent all my energies on making this happen for Syd."

Jake scowled while Marcel went into negotiating mode. "Jake, we made a deal. You're going to be able to speak and act through Syd and tell Samantha everything you couldn't before."

"What if I want to back out of the deal? Make a new one?" Jake asked. "We'll see what the council has to say about this. I'll appeal."

Marcel tried not to show his concern. The last thing he wanted was for Jake to interfere with his grand plan. The council heard Luis's testimony although, when he thought about it, they were not specific on who would take care of Samantha long-term. Marcel became worried. Would Jake challenge him in front of the council? Would he lose his chance to be with Samantha? Would they agree to let Jake return instead of him?

Without warning, Carmella burst into the room with long, dark, straight hair, a tasteful skirted suit, heels, and a matching sedate designer handbag. She looked like she had stepped right out of the pages of *Vogue* and appeared taller and thinner. She was almost unrecognizable.

Jake's, Mimi's, Bishop's, and Marcel's jaws dropped

"What do you think, guys? Don't I look like a million bucks?" Carmella asked.

She grabbed the controller from Marcel's hands and said, "Now, give me that controller; I think I know how to use this thing."

Mimi circled Carmella several times, studying her hair and clothes. Then she picked up the handbag and fondled it. She looked inside but it was empty. Carmella snatched it back and frowned.

"Looks like designer to me. I wouldn't mind a makeover and a new outfit, fully accessorized," Mimi announced.

Marcel motioned for Mimi to sit down. Carmella pressed a button on the remote and projected an image of Frank making out with the blonde.

"Don't like it, but there's nuthin' I can do about it. Knock yourself out, Frankie baby."

Mimi and Bishop laughed, while Marcel and Jake stared at each other. Carmella noticed the two flashing daggers.

"Okay, boys, knock it off. Mimi's right," Carmella said. "The Samantha and Syd thing is in motion. Look at this." Then she pressed the controller and an image was projected of Syd listening to Samantha singing, "*Let's Do It, Let's Fall in Love.*"

Jake stood up, alarmed. "Fuck, that was *my* favorite song."

"You wanted to speak to Samantha through Syd? Well, it's happening," Mimi said to Jake, folding her arms across her chest.

"We'll see about that. I'm going back down any which way I can, man, woman, pet, or child, and be with Samantha again," Jake announced.

Marcel looked concerned. He had to take action to prevent Jake from returning to Earth before him.

Chapter Eleven

More Good Phone

Syd bubbled over with enthusiasm after their first conversation. He felt a strong attraction to Samantha. Perhaps it was the idea of a woman twenty years younger. Most of all, she didn't sound like a phony. It was new territory for him to hook up with a woman who was younger, intelligent, and talented. He discussed it with anyone who would listen, including Damien, who had real concerns and no qualms about voicing them.

"Come on, Dad; she's probably a gold digger. Tell her there's no gold to dig."

"She's got her own money," Syd responded.

"You're thinking with your little head, not your big head," Damien said. "How old is she? Forty, my age?"

Syd corrected him and said, "Fifty", but Damien didn't change his opinion.

"Wait until she hears about your health problems. If I were you, I'd tell her real soon. She may run for the hills," Damien warned.

Syd knew Damien was probably right. He should've told Samantha about his heart issue and his prostate cancer, both of which were under control for the past two years.

There was one gnawing issue in Syd's mind—her weight. He hadn't seen a full-body picture and was determined to find out before too long. She was also cagey about how her husband died. Why was that such a sensitive subject?

He dialed Samantha's number and Bobby answered. He introduced himself politely and asked to speak to Samantha.

"Mom, there's a guy on the phone called Syd."

"I'll take it in the other room," Samantha replied.

Bobby was curious and stayed on the phone for a little while. He heard Samantha's voice soften to a purr.

He rolled his eyes, hung up, and said out loud, "It's about time."

Samantha told Syd that Barbara was having a get-together at her house and asked if he was interested in going. She had an ulterior motive: to get a face-to-face assessment from Barbara before she put any more energy into this phone relationship. She could trust Barbara—at least for the visual—but for the rest, she knew she needed her own up-close-and-personal observation.

Syd agreed to go to the party and arrived with flowers. He was shocked by how Barbara was so very different from Samantha. He could tell she was uneducated, loud, and obnoxious. He stayed the requisite amount of time, made an excuse about an early-morning engagement, and left.

Barbara made a comment as he departed, "Where are you going on a Sunday morning, to church? I thought you were a Jew."

Samantha was asleep the morning after Barbara's party when Syd called at 8:00 a.m. He was anxious to find out what Barbara had said. Syd knew the Barbara meeting was designed as a once-over. He knew he was under scrutiny and was dying to know if he passed the examination.

Samantha, of course, hadn't heard from Barbara, who probably stayed up partying till the wee hours of the morning and had a hangover; so she had no feedback to report.

Syd told Samantha the food was nice, but he noted, "The party-goers were vapid, superficial, and rough around the edges; not my cup of tea."

Syd got many points for this comment, as she was entirely in agreement. Barbara hung out with a lot of lowlifes and Syd was being kind.

Barbara called later that day and confirmed that he was a nice-looking, well-dressed, polite, amusing older man who drove a Jaguar convertible. Samantha then felt comfortable continuing the phone talk with Syd.

From that point, Samantha and Syd's good phone expanded from thirty minutes to one-to two-hour sessions. It became a daily ritual. By the first week, they had covered a multitude of topics. Some they agreed on and others not so much. On most issues, their opinions were not that far apart.

Syd lectured Samantha on his relationship theories and how men and women should communicate better. They spoke about business and exchanged ideas on markets and opportunities.

Syd described his door and window business while she listened attentively, asking questions. Samantha recounted her various positive and negative career moves while Syd commented on how smart she was.

* * * *

Syd started out his morning call with, "Good morning, my morning glory!"

Samantha sent him more of her vocal recordings, but Syd finally demanded, "I want live music! Sing me a morning song."

Then he asked for the lyrics by email so he could study them. Samantha tended to pick mournful ballads about lost love and heartbreak. Syd objected, forcing Samantha to choose carefully. Samantha also sent him love poems and remembered another couple who fell in love without meeting in person.

In the nineteenth century, the poets Elizabeth Barrett and Robert Browning had a long correspondence before falling into each other's arms upon meeting.

Samantha thought Barrett and Browning would be thrilled with twenty-first-century electronic communications. Imagine "How do I love thee? Let me count the ways," in a text message. They probably would've taken to Twitter and had millions of followers.

She still listened daily for any red flags, but Syd continued to make her laugh and was a very good flirt.

Samantha also had her gaydar turned on. She wanted to be sure Syd wasn't attracted to men. In retrospect, she probably missed the signs with Jake. Why didn't his obsession with the campy parts of the musical *Phantom of the Opera* raise concerns? Why didn't his deep knowledge of major Rodgers and Hammerstein musicals strike her as odd for a heterosexual man?

They did spend their first night together singing the entire score of *South Pacific*. Then there were the photos of naked young men, stuffed inside a girlie mag, she found at the back of his sock drawer. She dismissed it all and basked in her deep love and attraction for Jake.

Syd sounded convincing when he said he never had homo feelings. His preoccupation with women's love capacity helped him pass her gay test.

However, he became annoying with his insistence on a

full-body photo of Samantha, who responded, "Can you just take my word for it—150 pounds and five nine?"

Samantha wanted to knock off about fifteen pounds. She dieted and exercised so maybe by the time they met, it would be true. Samantha was concerned about Syd's phobia about personal appearance because it showed a sort of egotism. He could be a lovable narcissist.

She wondered what his girlfriends looked like or his dead wife, Mimi. He often spoke about Mimi's weight gain after they married and how unattractive she became to him. She felt sorry for Mimi, who was probably depressed and ate herself into an extra-large. Samantha had been there and done that. She wondered if Syd was at fault for Mimi's unhappiness.

Samantha was surprised Syd hadn't made any moves to come to Florida to meet in person. Was something holding him back? Maybe he was just an old wind-bag, stringing her along? He did say he was planning a trip to Florida imminently. He was aggressive on the phone and pursued her.

Syd had strong philosophies on love and relationships. He was adamant that a couple concentrate at least once daily on each other, if only for a few minutes. He had a rule that a couple should put aside all their worries and concerns and "At least once a day look into each other's eyes and talk about love."

Syd called it the "Love Meter" and he was convinced that once a couple could no longer do this, the relationship was doomed. He said he broke up with several women who refused to do this.

Syd pressed Samantha many times about why she didn't have a man in her life.

Syd asked her one day, "Do you use a vibrator?"

Samantha was taken aback. "Why would you want to know that?"

"Because that would mean you don't need a man," Syd responded.

"Many of my girlfriends have vibrators and still man-hunt."

With all her beauty and talents, he was surprised she didn't have a boyfriend. Samantha dodged the truth about why she avoided men and her fears of rejection. She was also concerned about Syd's reaction to her HIV status. He was older and probably didn't know much about it. He could easily get spooked.

Syd was equally reluctant to reveal his health issues. Damien kept hounding him and asking him if he had told Samantha.

By the second week, it weighed heavily on Samantha. She was determined to wait to tell Syd in person, if that should happen. She would take her chances.

* * * *

It was after hour fifteen of phone calls when Samantha received the job offer. As a courtesy, she called Lyle first and was grateful she got his voice mail. Then she called Syd to tell him her news.

"I got the job!" Samantha announced. There was no immediate reaction from Syd.

"Isn't that great?" she added.

"I am happy for you but sad for me," Syd admitted. He planned on spending the winter in Florida and looked forward to getting to know her. Now she was coming to New York to take a new job.

"Let's do a house swap," Samantha joked. Syd thought it a marvelous idea.

She sent him photos of the view from her beach front condo but still refused to send him a full-body shot.

Samantha investigated Syd's building, The Colony, online. It was a co-op and considered a luxury building. Samantha thought, *what if his apartment is a shit-hole?* Here was an unmarried seventy-year-old who liked shopping at thrift stores and flea markets for gadgets and knickknacks. He also informed her he had 186 clocks.

"Who cleans your apartment?" asked Samantha.

"Doris, the housekeeper comes every Monday. She's colored"

Colored? thought Samantha. She hadn't heard anyone say that since 1972.

* * * *

Their phone calls were now twice daily. As they made plans for the house swap, Syd became more excited about spending the winter by the ocean. He hoped it would bring back his childhood memories of Rockaway Beach. He felt he needed to be in the sun and on the beach.

He couldn't believe his good fortune—finding such a great,

good-looking woman with a beach condo at his disposal. He could sell doors and windows from there. He was convinced they could make the arrangement work.

* * * *

Samantha counted the number of coincidences and examples of common ground they had so far. It became alarming. They studied at the same university, Syd's factory was a mile from her high school, they both lost their young spouses in their thirties and raised young sons alone who shared the same birthday. They had close lesbian relatives, and were both non-coffee drinkers and nonsmokers. She felt that their meeting was orchestrated by someone or from somewhere.

She half-jokingly told Syd on one phone call, "Perhaps our dead spouses have a hand in matching us up."

Samantha added up the coincidences and wondered what it all meant. She decided it was time to consult with her astrologer, for her annual reading. She saw him for over twenty years and he had an uncanny ability to predict major events in her life. The astrologer predicted when she would get pregnant, a new job, and the month of Jake's death.

He also dished out advice on dealing with a horrible boss and said, "If I were you, I'd take Xanax."

During the reading with the astrologer, she didn't to mention anything about Syd; nevertheless, he did predict that a man was coming into her life.

He saw her with "a John-Wayne type, full of vim and vigor; a larger-than-life figure who will be very adventurous."

He also described Syd as a man who felt dead inside for a while.

"I feel dead and empty inside," said Samantha.

"Then it's a wake-up call for you both," he said. "Go for it!"

When Samantha told Syd about her reading, she was floored to find out that Syd had a lithograph of a young John Wayne hanging over his bed. What were the chances of that? Syd was also taken aback.

* * * *

As they hit hour forty of phone conversations, they imagined what an in-person meeting would be like. Samantha warned Syd that, although they got along so well on the telephone, there was no guarantee they would click in person. Samantha had fears that Syd would turn her off physically, and his touch would repel her. She refrained from projecting the future and hedged her bets.

"We have to be prepared that we don't connect in person," Samantha warned Syd.

"I can't believe that," Syd said. Was it desperation or conviction? Syd couldn't imagine they wouldn't have a deep attraction to each other.

"At the very least," Samantha considered, "we will be great friends with many shared interests."

"No pressure, Sam," Syd said.

He continued fantasizing about Samantha and held a firm belief she was the real deal. He was determined to consummate the relationship. He knew this was his last chance at love; his body and soul told him time was running out.

Somewhere around hour forty, Syd started to call her Sam. Only a handful of close friends and relatives called her that. She remembered Jake calling her Sam in the beginning of their relationship, but then he stopped; he said it sounded like she was a man. *That was ironic,* she thought after his death. That's how far in denial and in the closet Jake was.

After about hour fifty, they talked about sex. This was when Samantha became nervous. She held out telling him about her STD and went along with the phone sex talk for the time being. She was taking a big risk and knew it.

When Syd described his romantic plans for their first night together, his words sent shivers through her body, while Syd got a hard-on.

Then she asked Syd quietly, "How do you know I'm not frigid?"

Syd quickly responded, "Doubt it. Your voice, your looks, your eyes."

That is pressure, Samantha thought. She hadn't had sex for a very long time and wondered if she was still capable. She could also fake an orgasm and make him feel good.

Syd had his own worries, as he hadn't had a full erection since before his heart attack. Maybe he wouldn't be able to satisfy her. There was a Viagra prescription in his wallet. But he was afraid to take it as he heard some old dudes with heart conditions drop dead upon ejaculation. Despite all the fears, they continued talking about sex as if it were inevitable.

However, they still hadn't made any arrangements to meet. Samantha had an opportunity, as the new company would fly her to New York to find a place to live. This would be her chance to find out if there was something between them and if he would be gun-shy about having sex with her after she revealed her secret. She decided to be the aggressor and take action to arrange a meeting.

As thrilled as Syd was and convinced that he and Samantha already had something special, he was still plagued with doubts. Would his age and health conditions be turn-offs? He decided to spill all the details as soon as Samantha told him she was coming to New York.

"I need to tell you something about my health. There are things you may not be able to deal with," Syd said.

Samantha knew this was serious, as his tone of voice had changed.

He continued, "I'm okay now, but I had a heart attack and quadruple bypass surgery." Then he paused, waiting for a response.

"Any medications?" Samantha asked nonchalantly.

"Only baby aspirin. Sometimes, I think it was unnecessary surgery. I got sawed open for nothing," he said.

Samantha asked a few other questions about his symptoms and his diet. Syd was relieved but he still had to tell her the rest. "When I was in the hospital, they found something else," Syd said quietly and paused.

After five seconds of silence, Samantha said, "I'm listening."

"Prostate cancer," he said. He took a deep breath and held it.

Samantha wasn't alarmed by these revelations but relieved. It felt as if a huge weight had been lifted from her shoulders, and her whole body relaxed.

"Oh, I see. And the prognosis?" Samantha asked.

At this point, Samantha was half-listening to Syd, as she was gathering her courage to spill her whole Jake story and deal with the expected fallout. She was now free to reveal her issue.

Syd rattled on about hormone shots, his normal PSA scores, and his refusal to do chemo and surgery. He asked her point-blank if she had concerns and if this changed things.

Samantha immediately shot back, "Not at all, because I have my own life-threatening illness." Samantha said proudly, "Not only did Jake leave us bankrupt, he also infected me with HIV."

Syd relaxed now that he had gotten his revelations over with. He was half-listening to her. Samantha assured him that her condition was under control with a cocktail of the latest meds.

"So really, it could be a toss-up who would die first," she said lightly.

Looking at her photo, hearing her voice, knowing her successes—this couldn't be someone who would die of AIDS. It was probably all a misdiagnosis and untrue. He filed it away, 'compartmentalized'.

"I want to die in love," Syd announced. He clearly hadn't digested Samantha's revelation.

Syd had complete disdain for doctors and the medical profession, except for his old buddy, Saul Meyer who was an urologist. This doctor assured him he would never die from prostate cancer and Syd firmly believed it.

After their exchange of medical dramas, Syd and Samantha embarked on more intense daily phone conversations. This shared experience of life-threatening conditions was, by far, the most important to Samantha and convinced her their meeting had a purpose.

Syd, on the other hand, shoved all their respective health issues to the back of his brain and tabled them. He was just excited about the potential of having Samantha in his life.

* * * *

In the subsequent days leading up to Samantha's arrival in New York, the conversations lasted over four hours daily. The conversations flowed easily and freely.

They fantasized how their first meeting would be like. Syd didn't want to pressure her and offered her his second bedroom.

"I would be quite happy to kiss and cuddle you on the sofa in front of TV for weeks or months, until you are ready."

Samantha, on the other hand, was determined to find out in those first days if they had real chemistry. She was very clear to Syd, "We're not getting any younger. I'm starting a new job and we need to figure it out. We *are* going to find out in those first days if we have it or not."

Syd thought that was quite aggressive, but he did like strong, determined women.

Samantha added, "I can't play the dating game and start a demanding new job."

Samantha made a backup plan in case Syd turned her off at first glance. She would reserve a hotel room in New York in case it didn't work out. Then she would move out and move on.

At hour seventy, they started a countdown of how many hours were left before they would meet in person.

As Samantha packed her suitcases, she felt like a mail-order bride. *This is insane,* she thought, moving in with a man she had never met. She borrowed a box of condoms from her promiscuous neighbor. Veronica was her emergency call, in case Syd turned out to be psycho. Samantha would text Veronica every few hours until she felt safe. She didn't tell Bobby, Barbara, or anyone else in the family their plan. If it didn't work out, there would be no explaining to do.

Syd consulted with Judy and Damien about their plans. Judy was excited for Syd and proposed a double date with the new boyfriend she met online. Damien was still convinced Samantha was after a meal ticket. Syd assured him that she believed he was broke. In reality, they hadn't really discussed finances.

Syd went into action mode, cleaning up his apartment, buying new towels, and deciding what to wear. He planned their first evening out at a high-end restaurant. The next day, he would take her to brunch at a luxury hotel with live classical music. He also bought theater tickets and arranged to take her dancing. He would pack the four days with activity so that if he couldn't get it up, she wouldn't notice.

Samantha lamented the whirlwind of outings, as it was a shame she wouldn't be able to cook for him. Syd had a sudden rush of excitement. Wow, here was a woman who offered to cook, who wanted to "make dinner instead of reservations," as Jerry would say.

They logged eighty phone hours up until the two days preceding their meeting. Samantha became concerned as she suddenly realized Syd was always very loud, forward, and direct on the phone.

Is this guy capable of an intimate, empathetic voice? Can he take it down a notch or two? That would be critical for romantic chats.

Samantha broached the subject with him at hour eighty-one. On this last morning she called Syd, who answered the phone with the usual greeting, "Good morning, my morning glory."

"Syd," she said, "I'm worried that you speak on only one channel and at high volume."

Syd was perplexed and needed more details.

"I need to know if we can have intimate, soft conversations. Can you switch channels?"

Syd took a deep breath, lowered his voice and responded, "Intimate conversation is my middle name, sweetheart."

It still sounded aggressive to her, but there was hope.

* * * *

On the last night before Samantha was to fly to New York, they spoke for two hours and finally said good night at 10:00 p.m. After she hung up she went into a panic while Syd was feeling excited.

She couldn't go through with it. Her heart told her 'yes' but her brain was saying 'ridiculous'. She called him back a little before midnight and said, "I need to hear your voice. I'm very worried about tomorrow."

Syd remained calm and talked her off the precipice of doubt.

"Do you know why you are feeling anxious?" he asked.

"No," said Samantha quietly.

In a low, serious voice, Syd said, "Because you know that when you walk off that plane tomorrow morning, your life will never be the same."

Syd's words were enough comfort to give Samantha the courage to drag her large suitcases to the airport, board the plane, and move in with a man she had just spent eighty-four hours of "good" phone.

Chapter Twelve

Samantha and Syd

It was still dark when Bobby dropped Samantha off at the West Palm Beach airport. He wished her luck and then she hurried into the terminal. She was ready for action—clad in a short plaid skirt, a tight-fitting black sweater, a silk scarf, high-heeled boots, and carrying a leather coat.

Before boarding the plane bound for Newark airport, she caught sight of herself in a mirror and wondered if this was what a mail-order bride would wear. Why not? *It is an adventure,* she thought. It would be a great anecdote at happy hour and a good laugh with her girlfriends when Syd turned out to be a disaster.

* * * *

Syd woke up early, as he planned time to dress and stop at the market for a single red rose. He took his time, dressing in a gray suit and his favorite silk tie, and spraying himself with some Italian cologne. It was on the fruity side and for a moment he worried it smelled too gay. He didn't want to admit he was nervous but realized it when he misplaced his glasses and spent ten minutes hunting them down. He headed to the airport in his SUV, as the Jag would definitely not fit Samantha's luggage.

* * * *

Despite Syd's gentle pep talk the night before, Samantha was still anxious in flight and it was too early for a drink. As the plane reached cruising altitude and glided through soft clouds and a bright autumn sun, she relaxed. What was the worst that could happen? If she was repelled by Syd, she would make some excuse and spend the next four days in a fancy New York hotel.

If the meeting turned ugly or Syd acted scary Samantha would text Veronica who would call NYPD.

Even before the flight landed, Syd nervously circled the airport, waiting for Samantha's phone call. Samantha headed to the baggage claim, taking deep breaths. Once there, she collected her luggage, rummaged for her cell phone, and called Syd. He said he would be right there and to look for a black cherry SUV. She then headed outside into the crisp sunny air.

Unbeknownst to Samantha, he was already parked in front and was looking for her to emerge. He noticed her immediately, pushing a luggage cart, wearing large sunglasses, a leather coat, and boots. He jumped out of the car, holding the red rose, and approached her. She was looking at all the cars out front and hadn't noticed him. At first glance, Syd thought she looked like a movie star and much younger than he imagined. *Why doesn't she see me?* Syd worried.

"Don't you recognize me and my black cherry?" Syd said, facing her while holding the rose.

Samantha thought this funny but was taken aback. She shot back, "That's black cherry?" which was her way of hiding the shock that he looked so much older in person than in his photo. At least he was tall and well-built.

Despite the fact that Syd had planned, as he said, to kiss her on both cheeks as an initial greeting, he went straight for her mouth. Then he handed her the single rose. Samantha took it from him and then motioned to load the luggage.

After the suitcases were stowed, he rushed over to open the car door for her.

"Did I not tell you about my rule?" Syd asked.

"I just landed and you are already making rules?" Samantha remarked as she maneuvered into the passenger seat.

"You must always allow me to open the car door for you."
Quaint, Samantha thought, *and not a deal breaker.*

Syd slid into the driver's seat, then grabbed her hand and kissed it. As he drove away from the airport, Samantha asked playfully, using a heavy New York accent, "Well, Mister Weis, did I delivah?" Then she flashed him a smile and adjusted her skirt.

"Over delivered," he replied, glancing down at her legs.

Samantha then had an idea. "After eighty-four hours of marathon good phone, let's spend the next eight minutes and four seconds in silence."

Syd was concerned but went along with her wishes. He watched the car clock as the eight minutes slowly and silently went by. In those minutes of silence he thought this was a sure sign Samantha didn't like what she found.

Meanwhile, Samantha assessed the situation. Her eight minutes were spent reconciling with her decision, reasoning with herself: *If this guy wants to take me to a fancy dinner, the theater, and then to bed, why the hell not? He talked a good game, so let's see what he can do. What do I have to lose?*

After the car clock indicated eight minutes had passed, Syd asked, "Can we talk now?"

Samantha responded, "Four more seconds," and resigned herself to whatever would transpire. Syd was relieved when he could talk again and announced they were going to breakfast at his favorite bagel place in New Jersey. Samantha, told him only half a bagel for her. Syd saw this as a good sign: she was watching her weight.

Syd knew the staff at the busy bagel joint which was filled with sounds and smells of fried eggs. They were shown to a small table at the back near the restrooms, which was not conducive to conversation. They ate their bagels and left quickly.

As they walked back to the car, Samantha felt overtaken by force and kissed Syd smack on the mouth on the street. Syd was ecstatic at her spontaneous sign of affection. *Is this a sign of things to come?* he thought.

They headed to Manhattan through the Lincoln Tunnel. Samantha became nostalgic as they emerged from the tunnel. She remembered the days when she was a student—building a career and looking for lasting love.

They arrived at The Colony, where a valet took the car and said he would deliver the luggage. Samantha was impressed.

As they entered the fancy lobby, Syd acknowledged an older couple, dressed up and waiting for their car. Samantha heard the wife say to the husband as they passed by, "Must be his daughter come to visit." Samantha found this amusing but didn't say a word to Syd.

As he guided Samantha towards the elevator, he used military terms for directing: "Column right and column left."

As they entered the elevator and the door shut, Samantha had another urge to kiss Syd, this time for a little longer. When the doors opened on Syd's floor, one of his neighbors—a wheelchair-bound woman wearing a fur coat and hat was waiting with her Asian caregiver. Syd tapped the woman on the shoulder and said, "You look fabulous in fur, Margaret. Never take it off." The woman smiled weakly and the caregiver laughed.

They headed to his front door. Samantha noticed the *mezuzah* on the door frame and asked in a heavy New York accent, "*Oy*, Syd, have you checked the *tifilin*?"

Samantha wanted to impress Syd with her knowledge of Judaism.

"The what?" Syd asked.

"You know...the parchment scroll inside. My old neighbor says it's bad luck if it's crumbling."

Syd scowled and said, "Don't believe in those goddamn Jewish superstitions." He opened the door with his key, paused, and made a motion that he would lift her up.

"I guess I better carry you over the threshold."

Samantha giggled but discouraged him, afraid he would hurt himself. She entered his large two-bedroom apartment, which looked like a thrift store. She then noticed the 186 clocks that covered every wall and surface. She thought it was a joke when he had mentioned it. But there they were: old clocks, new clocks, cuckoo clocks, bird song clocks, digital clocks, a bowling clock, clown clock, ice cream cone clock, clocks with no numbers, and a grandfather clock. Despite the fact it was 11:35 a.m., every clock had a different time, but many were set at 10:10.

"Why ten ten?" asked Samantha.

"Look at any ad, they are all set at ten ten. It's the happy face."

Several clocks started to chime and Samantha was concerned.

"That does go on all day and night?"

Syd ignored her and said playfully, "Did I mention I have a romance with time?"

He took her coat and opened up the hall closet. He then motioned to the two large mahogany closet doors.

"Yours?" Samantha asked and Syd nodded. "Solid and very fancy," she added.

Samantha yawned. Syd grabbed both her arms and said, "You must be exhausted."

"I was up at four a.m. and we were on the phone until almost midnight," Samantha said. "I could use a nap."

"May I join you?" Syd asked casually.

"Sure, why not?" Samantha said.

Syd squeezed her arms and was about to kiss her when there was a knock at the door. They broke their half embrace as the valet arrived with Samantha's luggage. Syd instructed him to take them to a closet. He tipped the valet and ushered Samantha into a large, empty walk-in closet.

"All yours, my dear," Syd said. He turned on a light and showed her the built-in drawers.

"I did the same for you in Florida," Samantha said, fingering the hangers. "I'm going to change." She opened up one of her suitcases.

"Meet you in five in the bedroom?" Syd asked and walked away, adding, "It's almost noon; we have dinner reservations for six p.m."

Samantha really didn't care if he thought she was easy. She rummaged for the condoms that she took from Veronica. She had conveniently placed her silk Victoria's Secret bathrobe on top. She slipped off her skirt, hose, and blouse, and kept her underwear on. She wrapped herself in the black silk robe, stuffing a few condoms in the pocket. She was skeptical this would lead to successful sex, but at least she might get in a decent nap before dinner.

She wandered into Syd's bedroom which had a king-sized bed, the framed John Wayne lithograph, more clocks, and a wall full of family photos facing the bed.

Oh, Christ, she thought, *we're going to have sex with all these people staring at us?* Then she said it out loud, replacing the words "have sex" with "go to bed" so he could hear.

He didn't, as he was busy in the bathroom. Syd doused himself with more fruity cologne and stripped down to his white T-shirt and briefs. This was not his modus operandi, as he usually waited until the sixth or seventh date. He made an exception, given they were phone dating for five weeks.

Samantha slipped under the covers, still in her robe, and studied all the family photos from different eras. She figured out some were of his parents; his siblings maybe; his son as a baby, toddler, bar mitzvah boy, and graduate. Oddly, there were no photos of women—not even his dead wife.

Syd emerged from the en suite bathroom, slipped beside her in the bed, and fondled her robe. "Take this off; I want to see your body," he said softly.

She obeyed and he tugged on her underwear. She slipped that off as well as he undressed under the covers. Samantha was self-conscious until he said, "Just beautiful."

They were both naked and fell into an embrace immediately. Instantly, Samantha felt comfort and joy in his arms. It was so natural. Syd was shocked at the ease with which they came together under the sheets.

He began kissing her all over and felt her excitement as he explored all her general and private parts.

Samantha was so relieved that she felt enormous attraction to this man, who seemed to know what he was doing. A few weeks before, at around hour sixty-five, Syd voiced his concern about the possibility she wouldn't climax right away and said they would need practice. Samantha predicted if he were Mister Right in bed, there probably were no issues.

She was correct because less than five minutes into their first session, Samantha had an orgasm just from Syd's fondling and touches. Another climax followed, and then another. He hadn't penetrated her yet.

By the time Syd was partially ready for intercourse, Samantha was overwhelmed and had almost forgotten about the condoms. Syd seemed unconcerned about STDs. Samantha noticed he would get an erection, then lose it. Condom was not an option as it would probably slip off. It was going to be bareback.

Samantha was so turned on that even Syd's partial erection was sufficient for an orgasm. After she had climaxed over half a dozen times, Syd said, "Tomorrow we need to buy lube." He felt with lubrication he would be able to get an improved erection, maintain it, and maybe orgasm himself. He also complained about her "Brillo-like" pubic hair. Samantha felt embarrassed.

After a few hours, Samantha got up to go to the bathroom but also to grab her cell phone. She texted Veronica that she already had six orgasms. She was probably not going to a hotel.

Veronica texted back, "LOL. Assume he's not a serial killer. You go girl!"

* * * *

Syd had never in his lifetime been with such an erotic woman. He couldn't believe that, at his advanced age, it finally happened. He was deeply saddened that his performance was not up to par; Samantha deserved better. He determined to improve and keep her happy. He knew those damn hormone shots were to blame. Then again, an oversexed woman who required little stimulation was probably what he needed to wake up his half-dead cock.

Samantha was now completely convinced that somehow their relationship was being orchestrated. It made no sense but the journey had begun. Who knew how long it would go?

They both fell asleep and woke up refreshed as the sun set. They fondled each other all over again. Syd then ordered them out of bed to dress for their dinner engagement. They were going on their first date after they had sex.

Syd got up from bed, and Samantha noticed he proudly walked naked towards the bathroom. He asked her from the bathroom if his ass was wrinkled. He had seen an episode of *Sex and the City* where one of the characters, Samantha, fled the bedroom when she saw her new seventy-year-old boyfriend's wrinkled ass.

Samantha responded, "Relax, this Samantha reports no wrinkles."

Samantha stumbled through the living room, passing all the friggin' clocks, and into her closet to find clothes. After she showered and dressed, she went into the master bedroom to ask Syd to zip up her velvet knee-length dress. She avoided looking at the wall of photos and stared at the John Wayne lithograph. She felt in control and would not let one afternoon of delight carry her away.

As Syd zipped her up, he was hit by a wave of emotion. He realized he was madly in love.

Before they left the apartment for their first date, Syd said he had something very important to say. He took her hand and led her to the living room sofa. He beckoned her to sit down. This sounded serious, as if Syd was going to make a major revelation.

Samantha was curious and nervous at the same time. He took both her hands and kissed them. Then he looked into her eyes and asked, "Do you remember about the Love Meter?"

Samantha nodded. "Yes, you told me around hour twenty on the phone."

"You must promise that we will do this every day. In person or on the phone," Syd announced.

"Remind me again how this works?" Samantha asked.

"Simple. We sit and talk only about love," Syd said.

Samantha now felt bamboozled, but it seemed innocuous enough. This was important to Syd.

* * * *

They dined at an exclusive, intimate restaurant that had soft piano music in the background. Samantha impressed Syd by knowing all the lyrics to the songs that were played. Syd held her hand throughout the evening when she didn't have a fork in it.

"What did you think when you first saw me this morning?" Syd asked her while kissing her hand.

Samantha didn't want to tell him the truth and shot back, "I saw a tall distinguished man in an expensive suit."

"What did you feel when I kissed you?" Syd asked.

This sounded like a question a teenage girl would ask a boy, not an elderly gentleman to a menopausal woman, thought Samantha.

They returned to Syd's apartment and to bed for another several rounds of sex in new positions. At around 3:00 a.m., they fell asleep in each other's arms in complete amazement of what had transpired the previous eighteen hours.

In the morning, Syd grabbed Samantha, squeezed her tightly, stared into her eyes, and asked, "Who do you love?"

Samantha was taken aback, not expecting such conversation within their first twenty-four hours. She answered with a question, "Who am I supposed to love?"

He kissed her deeply and then stopped abruptly to ask, "Where's your tongue? Let me show you how to kiss, young lady." He thrust his tongue deep into her mouth, then withdrew. "That's how I want you to kiss me," he said to an uncomfortable Samantha.

"I'll work on it," said Samantha. Syd winked back.

They then headed to a pharmacy for a tube of lube. Syd was convinced it would help him stay hard. Samantha felt a little embarrassed and didn't want to show up at the checkout counter with only lubricant which was labeled personal warming lube.

She convinced Syd they should buy a few things besides the lube.

With the lube in hand, they walked over to the kitchen supplies and food section. Samantha loaded up the cart as she found absolutely nothing of value in Syd's fridge. Also lack of proper utensils that would allow her to cook him the simplest meal.

Without hesitation Syd pulled out his credit card and paid for everything. For Samantha this was a great surprise and relief to find a man who pays and was not bankrupt.

* * * *

Back at Syd's apartment, Samantha prepared lunch.

Here is a woman who not only has multiple orgasms with a simple touch but who can cook up a storm, Syd thought. He joined her in the kitchen, put his arms around her and said, "What did I do to deserve you?" They locked lips for over ten minutes.

* * * *

Mimi and Jake looked on in the viewing room with a mix of satisfaction and apprehension. The match was working, but maybe too well. Though they were warned about strong chemistry, watching it unfold was something else.

As Mimi observed Samantha chopping, blending, and stirring in the kitchen, she remarked, "She's screwing herself out of dinners out if she keeps this up." She pretended the affection didn't bother her.

As Syd took Samantha in his arms, Jake bristled and said, "This is what we signed up for, so we put up and shut up."

* * * *

After lunch, Syd and Samantha headed back to the bedroom for a nap and more sex. With the help of the warming lube, Syd got a little harder for a little longer, and Samantha had no troubles climaxing another half-dozen times.

"You're a sex machine," Syd announced. "It's unbelievable."

"Lot of catch-up," Samantha shot back. "So get ready!"

Syd held her and said, "What I really love about you is your mind; remember that."

"Great, I'll go with that," Samantha said as she leaped on top of him.

When they weren't exciting each other in bed, they had long conversations, usually in a spoon position or holding hands. Syd also liked to kiss his way and Samantha acquiesced.

Samantha was sure she had stayed detached and resisted thinking about the future or love. She was having such a good time, and the sex release was years overdue. They were fully intoxicated with each other until suddenly the magic broke.

On the fourth morning, Samantha woke up alone in bed. She wandered into the office and found Syd preparing a flyer. He was pasting a photo of an older woman with stringy, bleached-blonde hair, under words that read, "Dear Judy: Welcome home, my morning glory! It's your lucky day, sunshine!"

Samantha flew into a rage. She grabbed the flyer, held it up, and said, "My morning glory? Are you serious?"

Syd didn't respond but just looked at her quizzically with a knitted brow.

"What the hell! Do you say the same thing every morning to Judy?"

Syd still looked puzzled and asked, "What are you talking about?"

"You don't remember you would say, 'Good morning, my morning glory,' every time you called me?"

"I did?" Syd asked.

Samantha became worried and wondered if he was covering his tracks, or if he really had forgotten.

"You have no recollection of saying that to me?" Samantha asked.

Syd didn't answer her question but offered, "Judy is my neighbor and just returning from a visit with her daughter in Boston."

Samantha said, "This is not what you usually say to a neighbor unless ..."

"She has a boyfriend. She's a wonderful person. When I had my heart attack, she came to the hospital every day," Syd responded.

"Is this your routine? Recycle endearments? Not cool, Syd," Samantha said, folding her arms.

"What's wrong with you? She's eighty years old," Syd said.

"This does not make me feel special, not at all," Samantha said and stormed out, slamming the door of his office.

Syd followed her out to the kitchen.

"How can you say this?" Syd asked. "You're not special? Look at what we're doing. Living together after eighty-four hours on the phone? Didn't the last three days mean anything to you?"

"You're obviously not monogamous in your endearments," Samantha said tearfully. She composed herself and added, "What is she? Some sort of cougar, running after younger men?"

Syd went back to the office, and said loudly, "I told you she's an old woman!" He grabbed the flyer and brought it into the kitchen where Samantha was peeling fruit.

"Do you think I would go for her?" Syd pointed to the photo. He announced, "See? I'm tearing it up," as he shredded it in little pieces and dumped it in the trash. He added, "You see, it means nothing."

"Still doesn't make up for the fact that after a night of love, the first thing you think of in the morning is preparing a welcome-home poster for this Judy," Samantha said in a wounded voice without looking at him.

"Judy knows all about you," Syd said. "She can't wait to meet you."

"Do I want to meet her?" Samantha responded.

"I can't believe we're arguing about this," Syd said, sitting down. "What can I do to make it better?"

"I don't know," Samantha said. "I'm disappointed. I would never call another man by any pet name or endearment while I'm with you. It's emotional cheating. I feel humiliated."

Syd sat silent while Samantha pondered whether Syd had Alzheimer's or was just an asshole.

Chapter Thirteen

The Heavenly Council Revisited

The support group was crowded on the night Carmella had her trial run as the GPYF leader. Marcel had invited potential members.

The council changed the rules to not make the support group obligatory for guilty spouses who left young families. They now could either join the group and explore matches for their spouses left on Earth, or undertake rigorous spiritual training to become guides.

The council was concerned that twenty-first-century souls on Earth were in need of more guidance than ever. They were stepping up their efforts to develop more guides. The conundrum was that Earth souls were more sensitive to the spirit world than ever before, yet there were massive breakdowns and emotional crises. As with any successful corporation, they course-corrected to meet customer needs; in this case, customers were Earth souls in need of increasing spiritual guidance.

Carmella, in her smart new outfit and high heels, eyed the new recruits as they filed into the room. She approached Marcel and whispered, "If we were back on Earth, we would make a fucking fortune, finding matches for all these people."

"Marcel and Carmella's Celestial Dating Service," he joked. "Why don't you ask them for their credit cards?"

Carmella replied, "Stop! You're too much." She waved her hand, dismissing him.

Jake and Mimi were invited to address the support group. Mimi entered, still in her drab housedress, looking haggard, while Jake had a spring in his step as he arrived.

Marcel was suspicious. Why did he look so content? Jake approached Marcel and pointed a finger at him.

"We need to talk," Jake said.

"What about?" Marcel asked.

"The council," Jake said firmly.

"And?" Marcel gave Jake a puzzled look.

"I'm appealing the decision not to allow me to go down and be with Samantha," Jake said confidently. "They granted me a hearing."

Marcel tried not to appear concerned and motioned for Jake to follow him. He beckoned to Mimi to join them. He led them to the steps of the gazebo, which faced a night sky bright with stars.

"What's this about?" Mimi asked as they walked.

"Jake wants to go back down," Marcel replied. Then he turned to Jake and asked, "Do you really want to stop the Samantha and Syd match now, while it's in progress? It could seriously damage both of them."

"I'm going to save Samantha. You know as well as I, she's headed for disaster."

"I know what this is about," Mimi said. "I saw you squirming at those love scenes between them. It's like watching porn."

"Syd looks nothing like he used to. To you, he's a strange old man getting laid by a younger chick—my wife! Samantha looks almost the same as when I died," Jake said to Mimi.

Marcel put his hand on Jake's shoulder and said, "I warned you. Their compatibility score was off the charts and they were bound to have an explosive first encounter."

"It's hard to watch. She's so relaxed and happy with Syd. She's literally oozing sex from all her pores when she's with him," Jake said.

Mimi asked, "Was it not so hot with you two?"

"Fuck you. Of course it was hot but, as Marcel said, Syd and Samantha are off the charts."

"What are you going to change by going down there?" Marcel asked. "You won't go down as Jake Becker, the bankrupt banker with AIDS, but probably a friend, boss, pet, or hairdresser. You won't have a choice."

Marcel told a white lie here, as he knew the council was open to suggestions on incarnation, but he didn't want Jake to know that. He was now truly scared that Jake would win his appeal and ruin his plan to get back to Earth as Samantha's partner.

Marcel was doing everything by the book by allowing Samantha and Syd to fulfill their destiny. He would be patient and wait for his time. Jake was too anxious and emotional. Surely the council would see this and hold him back for spiritual development.

"I don't care. I need to be with her," Jake said.

"So, why are you telling me this?" Marcel asked. "Why don't you go there and plead your case?"

"I need your support as a character witness. Tell them how long I debated over Samantha's match and how much I care."

Marcel thought he had the upper hand and would be able to sabotage Jake's case, but then he realized he could risk destroying his own chances. He had to be thoughtful about his answer.

"How do you think they will react to a dead husband's fit of jealousy?" Marcel asked. "You need a compelling argument."

Marcel couldn't believe he was advising Jake when he should be sabotaging him. But he felt it was the only way to play into it.

Carmella came outside to let them know the meeting was about to begin.

"What are youse guys so serious about? Who died?" Carmella said, laughing.

Mimi piped up, "Jake wants to go down to Earth and rescue Samantha."

"What the fuck?" Carmella shot back. "You can't do it, Jake. Right, Marcel? You'll ruin the province."

"Providence," Marcel corrected.

Carmella responded, "It was in one of them fancy books they made me read. Yeah, Providence. Isn't that in Rhode Island?"

They all ignored Carmella.

"They agreed to hear my appeal and want Marcel as a witness," Jake said.

Carmella looked at Marcel and knew the dilemma he was facing. "Can't you write a letter of recommendation or somethin'? Does it have to be in person?" she proposed, trying to help Marcel.

A personal appearance by Jake in front of the council could destroy Marcel's plan, which she now knew involved hooking up with Samantha in the future.

Marcel ushered Jake into the night, towards the Heavenly

Council's chamber. They donned the obligatory white robes before they entered. Marcel was still unsure if he would support Jake in his plea or hose him.

As they entered the chamber, there was sound of New Age inspirational music interrupted by heavy drums as the doors opened for the entrance of the council. Marcel and Jake stood as the council assembled and the drumming stopped. A wafting of heavy sandalwood enveloped the chamber.

"They love putting on a show," whispered Marcel to Jake who sniffed the air.

"Performance art with smell o' vision," said Jake.

Marcel recognized the members as the same as his last audience. As Madame entered, she appeared at first to be the bejeweled female figure with upswept hair, dressed in an haute couture gown. Then Marcel remembered the council chief rotated, and after the hot blonde, it was now an elegant Asian Madame who sat in front of her nameplate.

She opened the proceedings, welcomed Marcel and Jake to the chamber, and read the rules. She asked Jake to state his business and provide a witness. Jake was nervous and looked to Marcel for guidance.

"Madame and distinguished council members..." Marcel began and paused for effect. "Jacob Becker would like to appeal the denial of his request to return to Earth to be with his loving wife."

The council members chatted excitedly among themselves. Madame banged a golden gavel that jolted them into silence.

"Mister Becker, this is highly unusual. We normally do not allow appeals. But Marcel has agreed to provide testimony on your behalf, I assume?" she asked, glaring at Marcel.

This was a pivotal moment because Marcel had to decide whether he would help or hinder Jake's case. Marcel cleared his throat while Jake looked on nervously.

"Your Excellency, I...I am prepared to speak about Jake's continued deep devotion to his earthly spouse, Samantha..." Marcel said, still uncommitted.

Madame interrupted, "I am confused, gentlemen. I believe this was settled when you agreed to a match."

Jake spoke up, "Yes, Your Excellency, but this match is most unsuitable. I wish to journey back and join my wife again."

"So, there is a match in progress and a destiny which you wish to disturb?" she asked in a firm tone.

Jake leaned over to Marcel and whispered, "Why does everyone here in the council chamber talk like constipated Victorian British assholes?"

Marcel put his finger to his lips.

Madame cleared her throat and continued, "There are other considerations and other souls involved. Knowing what you would propose, I invited the other party to testify."

The doors to the chamber flew open and in walked Mimi with a white robe over her drab housedress. She came forward, intimidated by the council. Mimi timidly approached the podium and the illuminated microphone.

"Miriam Weis, you have testimony in this case?" Madame asked Mimi.

"Yes, ma'am...I mean Your Highness," Mimi said.

Marcel, in a loud whisper, said, "Excellency."

"I object to Jake's, I mean Mister Becker's wish to alter the destiny of my Syd...I mean Mister Sydney Weis, and the match with his wife Samantha," Mimi continued.

"A decision was already made the last time Marcel was in this chamber, so we need a compelling argument, Mister Becker," Madame said to Jake with a piercing look.

Jake assumed that the previous council meeting was about the Samantha and Syd match and was completely unaware of Marcel's request to be matched with Samantha.

"The council has expended a lot of energy on this topic. These must be two very special people to get so much attention," piped up a council member dressed as a swami.

Marcel squirmed, as he expected Madame to reveal his request. Thankfully, Mimi derailed the proceedings by protesting.

"Your Highness, I mean Excellence or whatever, Jake is very jealous and can't stand that my Syd is so crazy about his wife."

"Is this true, Mister Becker?" Madame asked. "Are you jealous of your wife and her new partner?"

"I wouldn't call it jealousy, Your Excellency; deep concern and sadness. She's with a sick, old man who will bring her nothing but the same grief that she had with me."

"Don't buy that story, ma'am," Mimi said. "He's *green* with envy!"

"I'm very sorry to hear that, Mister Becker. You know, one of the first emotions we are supposed to dispose of up here is envy," she responded.

Marcel was happy the conversation was diverting to the ongoing Jake and Mimi feud and away from him. But would it continue?

"However," Madame continued, "there could be other factors I would like to explore. Marcel, as the match expert, we need your opinion."

The ball was in Marcel's court and Jake looked towards him with pleading eyes. Marcel hesitated, then said, "Mimi, I mean Miriam Weis has brought up a valid point. The match is in motion, and any change now would be problematic. But Mister Becker also has a valid concern that Mrs. Weis' husband is elderly and sick, and this could present a potential challenge to Mister Becker's wife."

"If that is her path, so be it," Madame said as the council members nodded in agreement.

"Surely, Your Excellency, is my Samantha supposed to suffer through two dying partners in a row?" pleaded Jake.

Madame was not moved. "She may gain from the experience. We have no sympathy."

Marcel then intervened. "I propose a compromise," Marcel said, but Jake looked upset.

"I'm listening," Madame said.

"That the current match continues uninterrupted and takes its course. The council revisits, at a later time, the possibility of Mister Becker returning to Earth to be with his wife again."

Marcel was taking a chance here and possibly sabotaging his plan.

Mimi said, "I can live with that, as long as my Syd gets what he's due."

"What about the testimony of the last council meeting?" Madame waved her hand.

Marcel waited for his hidden agenda to be blown wide open.

Madame read from a screen embedded in the table. "The notes here say that a witness was present to get assurance that Mister Becker's wife Samantha be taken care of."

"What witness? Who?" Jake demanded.

Marcel motioned for Jake to quiet down. "I'll tell you later," he said to Jake.

"Someone related to you, Marcel," she responded. "I'm confused. Can someone clarify? Who remembers the meeting?"

She looked towards the council members, who looked puzzled.

Marcel then whispered to Jake, "This is why God got pissed off and left. They're very disorganized."

This was a critical moment when any one of the members could reveal that it was Marcel who would go down to join Samantha. Luckily for Marcel, none of the members responded.

"So, apparently, no one paid attention," Madame said, looking to her right and then to her left. "I think that is a compromise we can live with. We will revisit this once the current match has fulfilled its course. I warn you, Mister Becker, you are to devote yourself to spiritual development and return here envy-free."

Jake nodded and bowed his head.

Marcel had bought himself time and could accelerate his plan while Jake was in development. Marcel, Mimi, and Jake waited for Madame and then the council members to exit the chamber.

"Why are they leaving? I was going to make a request," Mimi said in a disappointed voice.

"To order a new dress?" Jake said with a smile.

"*No!* I want to go back down and take care of Damien," Mimi said.

Marcel shook his head and said, "I wouldn't recommend it. Lost cause, I'm afraid."

Just as they were about to leave the chamber, Marcel noticed a note on his podium that suddenly appeared out of nowhere.

It read, "Padre Mateo, we have not forgotten."

Chapter Fourteen

Syd and Samantha Bond

Samantha moped for hours over the "morning glory" incident. It was obvious that Syd didn't get it. He looked at her, searching for a sign that she had either forgiven him or gotten over it.

Samantha prepared the table for lunch in silence and didn't look at him. The radio played Frank Sinatra singing *"Witchcraft."*

Syd approached her and extended his hand, inviting her to dance. Given that none of Samantha's former men knew how to dance very well or enjoyed it, she caved. He grabbed her waist and took her hand delicately. He danced her around the room.

As they passed all the clocks, Samantha felt a sense of peace and completeness. She realized Syd knew how to dance. As she surrendered to his lead, she let go of her petty jealousy and enjoyed the flow of their love.

He stopped mid-step and kissed her deeply. She responded and extended her tongue the way he liked. Then Syd knew he had her.

He asked her, "Who do you love?"

She resisted for a second, then responded, "I guess you," and added, "Who do *you* love?"

"You, of course, deeply and completely," he said with bravura.

He danced her back to the dining room table, and they sat down and had lunch. Samantha stayed quiet for a while, and then Syd took her hand and kissed it, asking, "How was our dance?"

"Lovely," she responded.

"You need dancing shoes," Syd said.

"What's wrong with the shoes I had on last night?" Samantha asked.

"Too low; you should have higher heels to show off those legs," Syd said, gazing at her legs under the table.

"Let's go shopping," Samantha said.

"Sure, but I have a surprise for you. I hope you won't take offense."

"Why would I take offense?" Samantha asked.

"It's a special treat. Judy knows a very high-end hairdresser on the Upper East Side. He's French."

"Really!" Samantha said, intrigued.

"I would like to treat you to a new hairdo. But if it upsets you…"

Samantha interjected, "Not at all. I always dreamed of going to famous stylist. I would be thrilled."

"Great. Judy will make an appointment. I think his name is Max."

Samantha swallowed hard at the mention of Judy's name; it brought back the morning glory incident.

"There's another surprise after that," Syd said. "It's not that you're not already beautiful, but I want you to look your absolute best."

"Let me guess. You're going to pay for a boob job," Samantha said jokingly.

Syd reached over and caressed her breasts. "They're already perfect. There's a makeup artist at the salon. I think she's his wife."

"Wow! That sounds fun," Samantha said.

Syd was relieved; he was afraid that she would be upset. He would never have dared to ask this of any of his other girlfriends. But Samantha was different: down to Earth, unpretentious, and adventurous.

Samantha took all this attention to her appearance in stride. It could have been interpreted as controlling and chauvinistic. However, Samantha could never remember receiving as many compliments about her physical appearance from any man or woman. She spent most of her adult years insecure and felt that it was all about to change. For all his quirks, and despite his age, Syd made her feel like an attractive twenty-year-old woman involved in her first romance instead of a borderline-menopausal woman a decade away from drawing on her 401(k).

Syd picked up the phone and called Judy, who immediately said she was coming over to meet Samantha. Within a minute, Judy rang the bell and Syd let her in.

Samantha stood nearby to greet her "rival" but realized immediately what a sad case she was. Multiple face-lifts had created a frightened expression and she had bald patches and a dowager's hump. She was warm and friendly, giving Samantha a big hug and a sloppy kiss on the cheek.

"I am so thrilled to meet you," Judy said loudly as if they were all hard of hearing.

Samantha suggested she make tea, and Judy accepted. As Samantha walked to the kitchen, she heard Judy say, "Oh, Syd, she's so lovely; better in person than her photo." Then she added in a loud whisper to Syd, "Don't blow this one."

"He's hooking me up with your French hairdresser and makeup lady," Samantha yelled from the kitchen.

"They'll make you more gorgeous, *bubbelah*. He's not cheap, Syd. I hope you're prepared," Judy said.

"I'll sell a few clocks," Syd said, laughing.

"What? This thrift-store garbage?" Judy piped up.

Samantha brought a tray with a pot of tea and cups. Judy studied Samantha closely as she poured the tea very carefully.

"Such elegance; you did well, Syd, and you deserve it," Judy said with a twinkle in her eye. She added, "I should be so lucky."

Syd looked proud and smiled at Samantha. Turning to Judy, he said, "You haven't done so badly: two rich and loving husbands."

Judy sipped tea, took a deep breath, and exhaled with a sigh. "They were good to me in life and good to me in death."

"I hear you're dating again," Samantha said.

"Arnold Levine, JDate number one hundred and fifty-six," Judy said proudly.

"JDate?" Samantha asked.

"Jewish singles," Judy explained.

"Arnold's seventy," Syd added.

"A cougar. I knew it," Samantha said, and Judy giggled.

"Well, he said he was sixty-two, but I pulled out his driver's license from his wallet after we had sex the other night. Or I should say, *tried* to have sex," Judy said nonchalantly. "The man's seventy-three and can't get it up!"

Samantha shot Syd a quick glance. He winked at her.

"Did you tell Arnold about the Love Meter?" Syd asked Judy.

"Leave me alone with that, already," Judy said. She made a face and shook her head. "If he could get it up once in a while, we could talk love."

Samantha laughed and Syd changed the subject abruptly. "Samantha, why don't you sing Judy a song?"

Samantha flatly refused and was insulted that Syd was treating her like a trained circus act, performing on demand. Judy saw Samantha was uncomfortable, intervened, and spoke about Chez Max.

As she drank the rest of her tea, she suggested accompanying Samantha to get the discount.

Judy had been a client for over a decade, ever since JDate number five. She got up, kissed them both, and called the salon to make an appointment for Samantha.

Samantha found Judy amusing and was reassured when Syd spoke of the older woman's history with an air of disapproval. Syd found Judy a pain in the ass sometimes but liked her attention. "She's not even worth an A to Z list," Syd said. Samantha look puzzled.

He then presented her with a list for her to read. It was titled, "Everything I love and admire about SAMANTHA—A to Z." Samantha would soon discover that Syd made A-to-Z lists for both personal and professional matters. He wrote them out on lined paper on a clipboard with a red pen.

Syd's A-to-Z list about Samantha had an adjective for every letter of the alphabet and, in Samantha's mind, ranged from accurate assessments to wild exaggerations regarding her physical attributes, talents, skills, and intelligence.

In Syd's mind, he couldn't say enough about Samantha. With each day, he discovered more favorable and endearing traits. He had fallen deeply in true love and, written in his own words, "for the first time in my life." Then he said it aloud.

* * * *

Back in the viewing room, Mimi became rattled by this revelation. Jake enjoyed watching her squirm as she heard Syd say he was in love for the first time.

"Don't forget, this was your idea," Jake reminded Mimi.

"These are probably the confused thoughts of an old man," she said.

"Doesn't change anything. He wrote it and said it out loud," Jake said.

Mimi paused and tried hard to say something to annoy Jake.

"What's it like to watch your wife have the best orgasms of her life with another man, huh?" Mimi asked Jake.

Jake hesitated, hid his jealousy, and responded, "I trained her well."

Marcel piped up, "She did have a good run with that Latin lover."

"I don't see Samantha making any proclamations about Syd being the love of her life," Jake added.

"Early days, Jake, my boy," Marcel said.

* * * *

Samantha was unsure of whether she was falling in love with Syd himself or with his love for her. She sensed that he knew this was his last shot and was throwing himself in completely. She tried hard to maintain emotional distance but kept getting drawn in. She decided not to fight it any longer and surrendered. They became intoxicated with each other after only a few days of cohabitation.

"Why do you love me?" Syd would often ask her. Samantha would list his positive traits but always begin with, "I love how you love me."

While Samantha dismissed the morning glory incident, she still had to contend with Syd's flirtatious nature in public. He also became obnoxious about the Love Meter.

It was embarrassing when Syd would start a conversation at a party with strangers. He would take a woman by her hands like he did with Samantha and explain the Love Meter and its importance to a relationship.

"You crossed the line with that woman at the party," Samantha chastised him.

"She was fascinated," Syd responded.

"I could see her husband was not. Didn't you see him rushing over when you were holding his wife's' hands?" Samantha commented. Syd shook his head.

He was conflicted about spending the winter in Florida at Samantha's condo. He didn't want to be away from her now that they were deeply attached.

Then again, Syd thought it wouldn't be a bad idea to have a break once in a while from oversexed Samantha. As wild as he was about having, as he said, "one hot piece of ass" in his bed, he was not sure he was up to the daily and sometimes twice-daily sex.

They also talked about selling Syd's condo and moving into a rental. Samantha was unsure if the job would work out and didn't want to make any long-term plans. She was adamant Syd needed to de-clutter his place before selling.

"All those clocks," Samantha began.

"Yes, I know. They all have to go," lamented Syd.

His gut told him to downsize and simplify—time to declutter and sell. They agreed on a plan to sell his condo and move into a smaller rental apartment somewhere near Midtown Manhattan to be near Samantha's office.

To Samantha, it was extraordinary that within days, they made plans together which took years for most couples. There was an acceleration of events and decisions which led Samantha to conclude that they might not have much time together. *Why are we compressing years or a decade of a relationship into a much smaller time frame?* Again, Samantha felt she had to play it all out to whatever the conclusion would be and that there was a purpose.

It did cross her mind that she could be faced with another sick and dying partner. Could she handle it? She estimated they would probably have at least five, maybe eight years together, given his cancer prognosis.

Syd's sex drive returned and he wrote an A-to-Z list called "Syd's Libido." However, he did get morose one night in bed and voiced his concern that there could come a time when he couldn't perform or satisfy her.

"We can always get creative," Samantha reassured him.

Syd grew more excited and potent every day. After only a few days, he had his first orgasm in years. He needed an oversexed woman to bring him and his penis back to life. Samantha continued to have multiple orgasms and, soon, Syd did as well.

One night, as they were lying in bed in afterglow around midnight, Syd's cell phone rang. It was Damien.

Samantha was apprehensive, as Syd had mentioned that whenever Damien called that late, it meant trouble.

Syd answered the phone, "My son, my son!" as if he were

giving him a virtual bear hug. Syd turned the phone on speaker so Samantha could hear the conversation. Damien's tone started upbeat but soon turned negative when he started describing his current uncertain situation. Samantha watched Syd's face change from elated to tense.

Damien was in Las Vegas, closing a real estate deal, and it sounded like he was involved with shady characters. His voice was slurred as if he were drugged or half-drunk. Syd ignored that and chatted with him about what he and Samantha were doing.

Damien said, "I guess you haven't told yet her you're practically broke, Dad."

Syd changed the subject. "I think I should sell the co-op."

"The real estate market sucks, but at least you'll get back your down payment. Wasn't that money *my* inheritance from my mother?"

"You don't know what you're talking about. I gave you that money years ago," Syd insisted.

"Negative," Damien said. After a pause he said, "You think you did, Dad."

"I have documented how much I've given you in your forty years. It's over a million smackers."

Samantha had seen the book containing photos and a detailed list of the over one million dollars accounted for in private schools, doctors, rehabs, bail bonds, and loans. He also had the A-to-Z list of Damien's traits in the book. They were not flattering.

"How long are you going to stay in Vegas?" Syd asked.

"If this deal goes through, I'm buying a place here," Damien said. "Lots of foreclosures."

Syd immediately thought it was not a good idea for Damien to live in Vegas with its many temptations. He had no fixed address and, until recently, was living in a friend's garage.

Syd recommended he contact his business associates in Vegas who were involved in construction. Damien wasn't interested and started on a monologue about his troubled childhood, the many doctors he'd seen, and the meds he was on. Damien's claim to fame was as a consultant for the movie *Casino.*

Syd would often tell the story of how he got the job by being approached by a producer while he was at the tables in Vegas. It was Damien's only accomplishment that Syd knew of, and he recycled the story repeatedly to new acquaintances and old friends.

After Syd hung up the phone, he remarked, "He's such a smart boy but always finds trouble wherever he goes. He called me from Jamaica once and wanted me to pay for a green card for his wife-to-be. Said she was pregnant."

"You mean you may have a half-Jamaican grandchild?" Samantha asked.

"I didn't know whether to believe him or not. After I said 'no', I never heard any more about it," Syd said and added that Damien called him a racist.

In reality, Syd was appalled by the thought of having a mixed-race or "colored" grandchild and daughter-in-law, but didn't want to admit it to Samantha.

Syd felt powerless to help Damien but wanted to stay involved. Samantha interpreted this as a father's deep disappointment in his only son, mixed with a degree of guilt.

"I'm not giving him any more money," Syd said. "He'd blow it at the tables or on drugs."

Syd hoped for years that Damien would straighten out and find his niche. He stopped advising him to stay away from drinking, drugs, and gambling, since he didn't have any influence or credibility with Damien.

"Damien is like someone else's child. All the mental issues of Mimi's family and...addiction like her alcoholic ex ,Mr. Garber?" Syd pondered.

* * * *

Back in the viewing room, Jake smirked at Mimi. "He's on to you."

"He has no proof," Mimi remarked.

"Just wait until Syd gets up here, then you're screwed." Jake responded.

Chapter Fifteen

Chez Max

Samantha was more than anxious about the prospect of having this Max, stylist to the New York jet set, touch her hair. What if he insisted on something dramatic and extreme like orange punk? She wanted a conservative, stylish hairdo and didn't want to end up an office embarrassment. Samantha had a reputation to protect as a serious middle-management executive.

"I don't want to end up looking like a New York chic freak," Samantha said to Judy as they headed to the Upper East Side in a taxi.

"Relax, hon. He knows his business," Judy reassured, patting her hand.

There was Syd to consider. He was very particular and direct. If he didn't like it, he would say so. Once this Max got his scissors going, she would've no control.

Samantha was also concerned about Judy. Her bald patches and scruffy look were not a good advertisement for Chez Max.

Syd was meeting them at the salon later to see the results and pay the bill. Samantha figured it would be no less than three hundred bucks a shot. She hoped he knew what to expect. Then this would be a good test of his spending comfort. So far, he had spent a bundle on entertainment and hadn't flinched. That could mean he either had plenty of money or was living on credit. Samantha decided not to worry about it.

Judy instructed the cab driver to stop on the 77th Street and Madison. They entered an older apartment building and Judy greeted the doorman by name as if she lived there. Judy directed Samantha to an elevator.

When one arrived, Samantha did a double-take, as she swore Tom Selleck got out. Did this Max just do his hair?

"Was that Tom Selleck?" Samantha whispered to Judy as they entered the elevator.

"Don't be surprised if you see famous faces up there. Max knows everyone," Judy responded. Samantha didn't think his hair looked that great.

It was an old-school elevator with an ancient elevator operator. When they reached the floor of the salon, the elevator man cordially bid them good day. The pretty salon receptionist greeted Judy in a French accent and knew right away that she was accompanying Samantha to her appointment.

A young male assistant with spiked, bleached-blond hair ushered them into a dark, intimate waiting area and asked what they preferred to drink: coffee, tea, champagne, red or white wine. They ordered tea. Samantha wanted to have all her wits about her when she was facing the unknown.

She upped her estimate to at least three fifty for Max to get near her head. They didn't wait long before they were both shown into the main salon, where Max was having an intimate discussion in French with a male client who had gotten a buzz cut.

Judy leaned over to Samantha and whispered, "He's the rejuvenation doctor to the stars, specializing in colon cleansing with juice fasting, coffee enemas, and high colonics."

Samantha gave the doc another look and couldn't imagine that this nondescript, wimpy guy with a buzz cut was important.

Samantha could see Max in the mirror. He was a fiftyish, mature, interesting-looking man around six feet tall, with short, graying hair, piercing blue eyes, and a slim build. He wore tight jeans, a fitted dress shirt, and expensive trainers. Samantha immediately thought he might be gay or at least bisexual.

He gave Samantha and Judy a quick glance and returned to his intimate conversation with "Doc Cleanse." Then, all coiffed, the doc rose from the salon chair, took off his smock, gave Max a kiss on both cheeks, and walked toward the reception area.

Max greeted Judy with open arms and pronounced her name in the French way, "Judith, *chéri,*" kissing her on both cheeks. Judy immediately introduced Samantha and Max also kissed her on both cheeks, greeting her with "*Bienvenue,* Samantha."

Samantha said a quick "*merci*," not wanting to get into any French conversation, as she was *tres* rusty since high school.

Max motioned for her to sit in the chair. He immediately put his fingers through her hair and started swishing her shoulder-length locks about. He looked in the mirror and, within seconds, announced in his heavy French accent, "I have a *vision*."

"Really, what is it?" Samantha asked as Max continued swirling her hair around.

The odd thing was that though her hair was dirty and hadn't been cut in months, it already looked great just with Max running his fingers through it and flipping it forward and back.

"I see nineteen fifties. Shorter and lots of hair in front, like Sophia Loren and Gina Lollobrigida. *N'est-ce pas?*" Max announced as he bunched her hair in front of her face. "No layers. It will take a year to complete *la vision*."

Samantha did the math quickly. At three hundred dollars a throw and if she came every two months, that was eighteen hundred a year. She doubted Syd would go for that.

Then Max summoned another male assistant who ushered her to the washing bowl. He gave her the most relaxing shampoo she ever had, including a head-and-shoulders massage.

Samantha heard Judy gabbing with Max about her boyfriend and his erectile dysfunction. Max laughed loudly and said, "ooh la la" several times. Max suggested Judy consult with another doctor client of his who specialized in such issues. "When zee equipment not working properly."

The assistant led Samantha back to the salon chair and Max went to work quickly, cutting away her layers and shortening her wet hair. He was done in less than ten minutes. Grabbing a blow-dryer, he proceeded to shape her hair with the styling brush. Samantha was shocked by how deftly Max worked. At that point, the cost was immaterial, as she was being transformed. Judy noticed and mentioned how Syd would be thrilled.

When Max asked who Syd was, Samantha told him a quick version of the story about the phone relationship and only having met in person a few days before. Judy filled in the details, including that they both lost spouses.

Max nodded knowingly and said, "*Eets destiny, chéri.*"

Then Samantha looked at Max and had a sudden epiphany.

"Maybe his dead wife and my dead husband fixed us up," she said, pointing towards Heaven.

"*Oy,* I just got the chills," Judy said, waving her hand.

Samantha gazed at herself in the mirror and ignored Judy's comment.

"It's a beautiful love story," Max noted as he coiffed her hair and then applied spray. He grabbed Samantha's shoulders and said, "A match made in Heaven. *N'est-ce pas?*"

He handed her a mirror to look at the back of her head. "*Voila!*" He then had an urge to grab and kiss her but resisted. Max just growled.

Samantha recognized Syd's deep, booming voice in the reception area. As soon as Syd entered, he flirted with the young French receptionist before asking to find out where Judy and Samantha were. Judy appeared and led Syd to where Samantha sat.

She pointed to Samantha and clasped her hands. Syd was amazed at the difference a new hairstyle could make.

"Baby, you look like a movie star!" he remarked. Judy introduced Syd to Marcel and asked him to look at her bald spots.

Syd held Samantha's hands and gazed into her eyes. Max observed them while half-listening to Judy explaining about her hair loss as a side effect of her incontinence medication.

Max/Marcel almost turned green with envy as he watched Syd and Samantha exchange an intimate moment. He saw live and firsthand what a >1000 chemistry looked like. It was electric and powerful. He was sure he would've the same connection to Samantha.

"She's not done yet. Camille is waiting for her," Max announced.

* * * *

Jake and Mimi observed Chez Max from the viewing room and were furious. Though the salon guy didn't look exactly like Marcel, but they knew it was him with a few alterations, like adding six inches to his height and dropping a few pounds. What was up with that phony accent? Since when did he get an Earth pass? Why was he interfering? What was the purpose? What was his agenda? Why did he need to connect with Samantha and convey the idea of the match made in Heaven?

How dare he?

Mimi was concerned that Marcel was disrupting the match, while Jake was disturbed that Marcel surreptitiously tried to get close to Samantha. Jake knew about the Lyle business and now this Earth visit was highly suspicious. This was about the only time Jake and Mimi agreed and they were ready to confront Marcel.

Jake was ready to lodge a complaint with the Heavenly Council. It might help his case to get back to Samantha on Earth sooner if they found out there was deliberate match interference. Marcel would have much explaining to do.

Then there was the girlfriend—Camille, the makeup artist—who looked like a slicker version of the new Carmella. What was she up to?

Camille, a tall, outgoing, late-thirties New Yorker, gave Marcel a wink and a nod when he presented Samantha. Camille commented on how ravishing Samantha's hair looked and led her to the makeup room while Judy and Syd sat in the waiting room, drinking tea and eating chocolates. With every bite of chocolate, Syd tried to avoid thinking of what it was all going to cost.

In the makeup room, Camille took Samantha's hand and directed her to a chair in front of a mirror. There were dozens of products lined up: brushes, lipsticks, creams, lotions, and potions, and a sign advertising the products: 'Beauty by Camille'.

"Prepare yourself, babe. When I get done, that guy out there won't leave you alone," Camille said, examining Samantha's face in detail.

"I think we're already there," Samantha replied.

"A little extra pizzazz won't hurt, hon."

"How did you and Max meet?" Samantha was bold enough to ask.

"Interesting story, but not as fascinating as yours, dear—moving in together without meeting."

Samantha was puzzled that Camille knew her story though she wasn't present when she told Max about her romance with Syd. Samantha changed the subject and asked, "So, how *did* you and Max meet?"

"In a grief support group," Camille said while applying foundation to Samantha's face with a sponge.

"I'm sorry, who did you lose?"

"No one, actually; but it's a great way to meet single guys." Camille laughed and threw her head back.

Samantha declined to comment and continued observing Camille color-match her skin to powders and blushes. It took almost an hour for her to finish. It would've taken less time, but Camille insisted on producing a face map with numbers corresponding to the products so Samantha could recreate the makeup easily. Then Camille filled a basket with all the products she had. Samantha eyed a sign about waxing and asked Camille in a low voice if she could help out with her brillo-like bush. Camille nodded, ushered into a room, heated the hot wax and stripped mercilessly. Within minutes and a lot of pain, Samantha's front looked like a five-year-old's.

While Samantha's new hairstyle by Max gave her a new look, Camille's makeover turned her into a knockout.

The makeover was free but the products clocked in at over eight hundred dollars. Max's styling fee was a mere two hundred fifty, but he insisted on a fancy French hair-dryer and specialized hair products. That added another two hundred to the bill. Camille must have thrown in the "bush" removal as a bonus. Syd didn't flinch and handed over his credit card.

Samantha was so dizzy by the end and mesmerized by her new look that she didn't protest during the product-selling blitz. It wasn't until later that she felt guilty about Syd laying out such a big chunk of change. She wasn't sure he could afford it.

Syd reconciled that it was the price for having a trophy girlfriend. He did make Samantha promise to follow Camille's instructions daily. He already planned to make copies of the face map and tape them to both bathroom mirrors, with a spare copy for her Florida condo. This was a big departure for Samantha, who wore relatively little makeup. She would have to get up an hour earlier every day for the ritual.

Syd took a slew of photos of Samantha in the hotel lobby and outside the hotel on the street. Judy hailed a taxi and took off for her advanced Kabbalah workshop, while Syd and Samantha strolled down Madison Avenue, window-shopping. They walked at a slow pace; holding hands, until Samantha stopped in front of a shoe store window. She pointed to high-heel shoes with straps and asked, "Dancing shoes?"

Syd nodded and they went in. She tried on the shoes in her size and then Syd motioned for her to stand. Samantha knew it meant he wanted to dance, so she started singing "That Old Black Magic" in swing style. He took her hand and they danced around the shop while the assistants applauded. At that point, Samantha knew whatever the shoes cost, she'd have to buy them. They stopped in front of the register and had a long, deep kiss. Samantha made sure to use her tongue.

Then Syd whispered in her ear, "I've got a hard-on."

Samantha whispered back, "This may help keep it hard."

She took Syd's hand and guided it under her skirt and underneath her panties to feel her newly shaven hoo-ha. "No more Brillo," she said. Syd broke into a smile as he caressed her bald front.

He felt like the luckiest guy alive with a beautiful, younger woman at his side, who showed him pure love and no bullshit. She shaved just for his pleasure. It was a miracle!

Samantha thought about what she had blurted out to Max about being united by their dead spouses.

Could it be possible that Jake and Mimi had a hand in this? Do the dead have such power? Why was their relationship so intense and accelerated?

* * * *

Mimi and Jake waited for Marcel and Carmella to return. They wanted an explanation for his interference. Also, how did Marcel and Carmella get to whiz down to Earth for a quickie? They felt cheated all the way around. Marcel and Carmella were having all the fun while Jake and Mimi watched their spouses engage in this hot and sexy romance. This made no sense. Marcel had a hidden agenda and Carmella was his accomplice.

Marcel and Carmella entered the gazebo, giggling about their sojourn to Earth.

"That French accent was too much. You ought to be an actor," Carmella remarked to Marcel.

They found Mimi and Jake sitting on the sofa in silence, looking at them distrustfully.

"What, no fighting? Did you both finally kiss and make up? Awfully quiet," Marcel remarked.

"You two look like you had a good time," Jake said.

"Yeah, messing with our match," Mimi added.

"Messing? We were solidifying," Marcel announced.

"It was fun but I kind of missed being up here with you guys," Carmella said.

Marcel sent them out of the viewing room, claiming he had new matches to make.

In reality, he would try an experiment. He was testing out his compatibility with Samantha. As a dead soul, he couldn't measure his CM. He would go with his intuition that there would be chemistry no matter how he was sent back to Earth.

Chapter Sixteen

Syd Downsizes

Syd called Wanda, a Realtor who sold many units in The Colony and former girlfriend of Jerry Feingold. He and Samantha met with her. He wanted her opinion on what his co-op was worth.

Wanda, a stylish blonde model of yesteryear, breezed into the apartment in a calf-length mink coat and leather high-heel boots, fully accessorized and carrying a LV handbag. As thrilled as Wanda was with the fabulous view looking east, she was equally appalled by the clutter.

"You did all right, Syd, for a change," Wanda remarked while looking at Samantha up and down. Then she wandered from room to room.

"She's a bitch. Took her last husband to the cleaners," Syd said to Samantha in a low voice.

"Jerry dodged a bullet," Samantha said.

"He says she's completely bald under that wig," Syd quipped.

As Wanda finished her walk-through Samantha fixated on her hair.

"In this condition, you will never sell. Call me when you get your act together," Wanda announced and floated out of the apartment.

Syd made a face behind Wanda's back as if she is crazy and then giggled pointing to her head.

Samantha ignored him, then shook her head . She refrained from saying, "I told you so."

* * * *

Syd went into action mode, determined to sell his co-op. He first made his A-to-Z list of the furniture they should keep for their new, smaller apartment and items to go to Florida. He was so motivated to downsize, simplify, and reduce his financial burden, he decided to hold an estate sale to get rid of the clutter.

Syd called Damien and ask if he wanted anything. Damien declined, saying in his nastiest tone, "What? You mean *that* junk?"

Then Syd contacted his niece, to see if she wanted to sell the clocks and earn a commission. Alana and her partner decided to drive to Manhattan and see for themselves.

When the middle-aged lesbian couple arrived, it felt like black clouds of negativity had entered the room. They were busted out and looked it. Alana's four-hundred-pound girlfriend, Fiona, barely fit through the doorway.

They were both unemployed and living free in someone's basement. Alana had a job in a warehouse but hurt her back carrying boxes and was seeking disability. She talked about the brain tumor she supposedly had for the past two decades and added that Fiona needed knee surgery.

Syd tried to sound concerned but was visibly detached during the visit. He also avoided any discussion of money. Alana and Fiona couldn't be bothered with the clocks. When she realized Syd was not going to give her a handout, Alana took family photos and left.

After failing to sell the clocks to a dealer, Syd gave them away along with the knickknacks. Samantha allowed him to keep favorite clocks, preferably the ones that didn't chime. Syd reminded her of his "romance with time." They held an open house and invited all the workers and co-op residents to take what they wanted.

Once the last visitor left with an armful of stuff, Syd collapsed into an overstuffed chair and said, "Well baby, we're almost there. We make a great team."

Samantha didn't want to dampen his mood, but after the great giveaway, there was still a lot of stuff remaining. She sat on his lap.

He kissed her deeply and said, "You see; I'm getting a hard-on." Samantha looked skeptical as she usually did. "You don't believe me, do you?" he asked.

"Words, words; I like action," Samantha said playfully. Samantha's idea of a hard-on was much different than Syd's.

* * * *

Over the next few weeks, Syd hired workmen to do repairs and painting. Samantha tried her best to touch up the kitchen and bathrooms with tasteful accessories. Then they hauled off the rest of the junk to the Salvation Army. Syd was on a mission and threw out decades worth of paper, sorted photos, and gave away his old clothes. After a month, the co-op was transformed from clutter to clean, white, empty walls; a few decorative pieces and basic furniture; with all personal items hidden away.

Then one day, as they were putting final touches on the bathroom, the phone rang. It was another Realtor, who had seen the apartment before Wanda and wasn't so bothered by the clutter. Janine had eager clients looking at other units in the building. She asked if she could come by in the next half hour.

Samantha swung into action, tearing the tags off the towels and mats, turning on all the lights, putting down the toilet seats, smoothing the bedspread, putting on classical music, and spraying lavender air freshener around the rooms. Then Samantha announced in a heavy New York accent, "Okay, Mister Weis, it's show time!"

Janine was as scruffy as Wanda was polished. A petite, dark-haired, forty-five-year-old realtor in a baggy wool overcoat, she escorted an older couple through the door. Janine looked like she had just gotten out of bed and reeked of cigarette smoke. Samantha had never seen a Realtor look so ratty.

Syd, the consummate salesman, went about selling the co-op like he did his doors and windows. He pointed out all the features, recounted the history of the building, and name-dropped semi-famous current and former residents. He proudly showed them the view to take their minds and eyes off the dated kitchen, appliances, and bathroom fixtures.

He used the term "original features." In Samantha's opinion, they were just old. She often remarked that they could film an episode of *Mad Men* in the kitchen and not have to change a thing.

The Colony was constructed in 1965 and, although Syd bought it in the late 1990's, he hadn't spent a dime on updates.

Much to Samantha's surprise, the prospective buyers spent less than fifteen minutes touring the co-op and made a decent offer later that evening. Syd was thrilled, though he would probably realize a profit of only ten thousand dollars. He had done it—downsized and de-cluttered his life.

They celebrated in bed with chocolate-covered strawber-ries, followed by the usual hot sex. Syd only allowed her two strawberries as he was concerned about her weight.

The next day, he was adamant they take a day trip to Rockaway. Syd wanted to show her his family home, the soda fountain, and the beach where he played as a child. Then he took her to the exact place where he wanted his ashes spread when he died. Samantha thought it odd and sad that, at age seventy, his happiest memories were of childhood.

With the co-op sold, Syd's new mission was getting to Samantha's condo in Florida for the winter. In preparation, he visited his oncologist for a hormone shot. He reported back to Samantha that everything was fine, which was a lie.

Syd was in deep denial. The oncologist said he needed to change treatments, as his prostate cancer was progressing. He made several suggestions and Syd rejected all of them. He preferred listening to his old friend, Saul Meyer. The urologist always maintained Syd would never die from cancer. Syd chose what he wanted to hear and tuned out the naysayers. He felt all he needed was to bathe in the sun, the ocean, and Samantha's love. It would be his treatment plan and cure.

Though Samantha's job became more demanding, she flew down to Florida every few weeks to be with Syd for a long week-end. Once the warmer weather arrived, Syd returned to New York. They settled into a new apartment and enjoyed the city.

"I think I can cope with being away from you, but it's going to be hard," Syd said. They would still have the phone, which they were good at, or Skype with the computer hooked up to the flat-screen TV—that was, if Syd could figure it out.

Bobby was preparing to leave for college and was already half-moved out of the Florida condo. He was fine with Syd spending the winter. Bobby and Syd would be roommates for a few weeks before he went off to college. He offered to move his desk into Samantha's office so Syd could sell doors and windows.

Syd was a little hesitant and skeptical, as he said Bobby did "bad phone" the first time they spoke. However, Samantha knew Bobby was a well-behaved and polite young man who would make Syd feel welcome in their home. The second time Samantha put Bobby on the phone, Syd was pleased and pro-nounced, "He did good phone."

* * * *

Syd packed up his Jaguar with as much stuff as he could, including several clocks, a small carpet, radios, clothes, files, and his A-to-Z lists, as well as his door and window catalogs. Samantha was impressed with the energy he showed during this process. She proposed driving down with him, but Syd was concerned it would jeopardize her new position and insisted on going alone.

On the morning of the departure, Syd woke up at 6:00 a.m. The expectations of getting to Florida in his Jag made him so excited with a real hard-on that he woke Samantha and then leaped on top of her. She had her usual multiple orgasms within minutes; it was unusual for Syd to choose a missionary position. He was extremely energetic that morning.

He announced, "action," rolled off her and headed back to the bathroom for a shower. He dressed quickly and called the doorman for his Jag.

Samantha was very concerned about him driving alone all the way to Florida. He told her how he was stopped by a Georgia state trooper for speeding. The consummate salesman spun a story about his buddies in the NYPD and showed him an old receipt for his generous donation.

"Didn't you say that receipt was from 1973?" Samantha asked.

"It's been photo-copied so many times you can't see the date anymore." Syd laughed.

Syd was taken aback by the breathtaking view of the ocean from Samantha's condo. His body and soul relaxed immediately. He didn't miss his clocks anymore.

Samantha's place was everything Syd expected and more. Bobby welcomed him with pizza and Coke.

"Here's to a happy, warm winter." Bobby toasted Syd with his Coke can. Syd smiled but then turned serious.

"Listen to me carefully," Syd said to Bobby in a stern voice. "Your mother's counting on you to do well in college. No funny business."

Bobby wasn't sure what Syd meant but clinked his Coke can again with Syd's. He was happy his mother finally found a nice companion and was unconcerned about the age difference. Syd seemed like a nice guy.

They fell into a routine over the next few weeks. Bobby was working full-time at the supermarket to make extra money for college. He would often call Syd before he left work and ask what he wanted for dinner. They ate dinner together most nights; Bobby usually cooked. Bobby, serious and responsible, was the polar opposite of Damien. Syd complimented Samantha on what a good job she had done raising her son and wondered how he went wrong with Damien.

Syd encouraged Bobby to go out and questioned him on girls. Bobby didn't have much to say except that dates cost money and he was saving.

One evening Bobby said he was coming home late. Syd thought it sounded like he had a date. Syd excitedly called Samantha, who was in London, to tell her the good news. Samantha knew very well where Bobby was but was reluctant to tell Syd. As Syd carried on about the importance of Bobby having a love life, Samantha interrupted.

"I know where Bobby is tonight and it's not with a girl," she reported.

"Really. Where? Why didn't he say?" Syd asked.

"He didn't want to upset you," Samantha said.

"Why? Is he all right?" Syd asked, concerned.

"Bobby is at the Miami city morgue," Samantha announced. She hesitated and continued, "He's identifying Alfonso's body, which has been in the cooler for weeks."

"What?" Syd asked.

"Alfonso, my ex. He was found dead from a heart attack at fifty. Very sad. He lay on the floor of his rented room for six days. Apparently nobody cared enough to check on him until the landlord wanted him to move his car. They called Bobby."

"Why Bobby?" Syd asked.

"It appears Bobby is his executor and only heir. Alfonso's rich family in Argentina is pissed."

"What?" Syd exclaimed.

"Despite the fact Alfonso verbally abused Bobby daily, apparently he loved him," Samantha said.

"How do you feel about his death?" Syd asked, concerned.

"Nothing. The guy was a nut job," Samantha responded and added, "Bobby is also detached. In fact, he called me from the morgue after he identified the body. Bobby found a Starbucks card in Alfonso's wallet and he was on his way for a victory drink." Samantha ended with a giggle.

Syd didn't find this funny but Samantha wanted to prove the point that neither she nor Bobby felt anything for Alfonso anymore. She decided not to tell Syd how Bobby jokingly said about Alfonso's manner of death, "That's what you get when you take away my video games,"—referring to a horrible incident when Alfonso, in a manic rage, stormed into Bobby's room and removed his Nintendo and all his video games for no reason.

Samantha mentioned in a cheerful voice, "Bobby also found a pair of Miami Dolphins tickets for next week in the wallet!"

When Bobby came home later that night, Syd said, "Sorry for your loss."

Bobby shrugged and responded, "The guy was an asshole."

Syd figured that Alfonso must have treated him very badly and dropped the subject.

Before going to bed, Bobby asked Syd to go to the Miami Dolphins game with Alfonso's tickets. Syd made the mistake of telling Damien, who flew into a jealous rage and hung up the phone, after saying, "You never took me to any goddamn game!" Syd failed to tell Damien that he didn't buy the tickets and that they came from a dead man's wallet.

Damien immediately called Samantha and warned her in a quiet, sinister voice, "It may not be such a good idea, having Dad hang around with your son."

At first, Samantha wasn't sure what he meant and asked Damien to spell it out.

"Dad may not have told you what happened when I was a teenager."

She then remembered that Damien had made accusations of molestation in the past but then recanted, admitting he may have imagined it. Syd had shown her a doctor's report, which stated that Damien suffered from delusional behavior, possibly prompted by hallucinogenic drug use or schizophrenia. It was unthinkable that Syd was a child molester. She was convinced Damien aimed to hurt Syd in the worst possible way. She wondered why Syd continued his relationship with Damien after the accusations. Was Syd's guilt so deep he could forgive Damien for putting him in the position of being falsely arrested for molestation?

Samantha politely steered the conversation to another topic and then hung up the phone. She was shaken more by Damien's vileness than by his accusation.

* * * *

Mimi was horrified by her son's behavior and held her breath when she observed him trying to sabotage Syd and Samantha's relationship. As much as she hated to ask Marcel for favors, she did ask whether he would intervene and ensure that Samantha didn't get cold feet. She tried to make sure Jake didn't hear about Damien, but he overheard the scene and flew into a rage. He was against the match anyway and now his son was in danger.

"You know it's not true, come on, the guy is unhinged," said Marcel reassuringly.

"What were you thinking, man?" screamed Jake.

"Calm down. She's smart and will see right through it," Marcel assured him.

"I have to admit, this threw me," said Mimi.

"Look you two, their bond is strong. You've seen it."

Jake and Mimi both nodded. Marcel convinced them the relationship would go the distance. At least this was what Marcel hoped. There were now new variables and he was winging it.

* * * *

Samantha didn't have to ask Bobby; she knew it was a bullshit accusation. Damien was a sick fuck and wanted to sabotage Syd's happiness. When she told Syd what Damien had said, he went silent and 'compartmentalized'.

Syd said he would take care of it, but it was unclear what he meant. Syd's reaction was to call Jerry the lawyer to update his will and documents. Jerry knew Syd had no other choice and didn't discourage him from granting Samantha power of attorney and making her the executor and main beneficiary of his will. He purposely left Alana out and designated a small sum and the Jag for Damien.

When Samantha arrived in Florida the first time since Syd moved in, she saw how comfortable, tanned, and relaxed he was. He had the few clocks she allowed him, a functional office, and his favorite spot on the deck overlooking the ocean, where he would do good phone.

He hung his diploma next to hers. Since they were from the same university, they looked identical in font and format. He hung framed photos of Samantha after her new hairdo and makeover at Chez Max. He hung a painting of himself as an eighteen-year-old after his high school graduation that Estelle had commissioned. He also brought the John Wayne lithograph to hang beside his desk.

They played in the ocean, walked on the beach, danced in the pool, and held a party for friends, neighbors and his cronies from Far Rockaway High School. Syd was so proud of Samantha.

"I'm going to buy you something really special," Syd said near her birthday.

When the day came, they went out dining and dancing. He presented her with a card and flowers. After a few days, he changed his mind and announced that he thought his love, the dinner, flowers, and card were sufficient. Samantha felt Syd treated her as if they were in a casual relationship, and not living together.*Was he in his right mind or was he suddenly becoming miserly, or both?*

* * * *

Several weeks later, it was Damien's fortieth birthday and Syd asked Samantha what to buy him. She was flabbergasted that Syd would contemplate spending a dime on her son.

She almost became visibly upset but composed herself and replied, "Why don't you buy him the same thing you bought me for my birthday." Samantha paused, then said, "Which was nothing."

Syd was puzzled at this comment. Then he thought long and hard. He was certain he had bought Samantha a birthday present. He then remembered the conversation about the dinner, the card, and the flowers. He announced they were going to a jewelry store that afternoon to buy her a birthday gift. Samantha had conflicting feelings about wearing a guilt present. She went along with it and reluctantly chose a bracelet. She was considerate to not choose a very expensive one, as she was now well aware Syd had limited resources.

She was more annoyed when, a few weeks later, Syd asked, "What should I buy Alana for her birthday? Maybe I should get her new clothes for job interviews."

"The woman's probably not interested in dressing for success," Samantha said. "She obviously needs cash. Buy her a grocery store gift certificate."

Samantha found Syd's judgment flawed in so many areas,

especially with regard to his family. The only ones he finally gave up on were Murray and Fran.

They lived in Delray Beach, only a few miles from Samantha's condo, and invited Syd for dinner one night. They proceeded to dredge up old arguments from forty years before and continued blaming him for their daughter Alana's predicament and her becoming a lesbian. Syd had continued his contact with Murray only as a promise to his mother. Now he couldn't fulfill that promise any longer.

* * * *

Samantha returned to Florida several more times that winter and spring. Syd would pick her up in the red Jag with the top down.

She noticed he walked more slowly. When they walked together, he could no longer keep up with her pace.

One day, as they went into the ocean, Syd said, "Hold me, baby, so I don't fall."

He often had aches and pains and sometimes spent the entire day in bed. Samantha massaged him, applied hot compresses, and held him at night like a child. She tried to steer him towards a healthier diet and encouraged him to take vitamins and supplements. She noticed he dropped twenty pounds since they first met, only six months before. She was alarmed and begged him to see new doctors if he didn't like the old ones.

"Why are you so good to me?" Syd would ask and then kiss her hand. Though she felt deeply connected to him and gave him all her love and tenderness, it felt like Jake all over again. She was also worried about his unbalanced family and the prospect of dealing with them should he get seriously ill.

Syd was devastated when she said, "Syd, you've aged twenty years since we met."

Samantha hoped this would propel him to get stronger but then added, "I'm here to help you." In reality her thoughts drifted toward an exit strategy.

Chapter Seventeen

Heavenly Intervention

"I'm doing this for you, baby," Syd said in a child-like voice as he lay on a doctor's exam table. Samantha stood by him, holding his hand. She looked down at him with care and concern in her eyes.

"Treatment, no treatment—whatever you decide to do, you need to believe in it. I'm here for you," Samantha said lovingly. She immediately remembered those were the same words she had said to Jake shortly before he died. She decided to skip the next part: *Am I healing you into life or into death?*

"My love, my love," Syd said, lifting her hand to his mouth and kissing it. "What did I do to deserve you?"

Syd checked into the Cleveland Clinic in downtown West Palm Beach. He spent several days there while a team of doctors poked, prodded him and performed multiple tests.

He finally allowed Samantha to see his test results and treatment plan. She was not surprised to read in the reports that he had advanced cancer and needed aggressive treatment. The only treatment he agreed to was a blood infusion, as he was severely anemic.

Samantha couldn't help but sob in bed every night once Syd was asleep. *What happened to that vibrant and energetic man? What did I sign up for?*

When he heard her crying one night, he said, "You don't deserve this. You're young and beautiful and should be with a healthier man who can give you what you need."

Despite being conflicted about taking care of a very sick man, she still felt attached to Syd. For his seventy-first birthday, she bought him an expensive watch and prepared an A-to-Z list with all the traits she loved about him. He teared up as he read the list and then asked if she could read it to him out loud.

She took him to a pricey restaurant where she arranged to sing a few tunes with the resident jazz trio. She sang all of his favorite ballads. He was so proud of her and couldn't stop taking pictures. Syd rallied that night with enough energy to dance the Lindy and have sex.

They remained in bright spirits until Damien called to wish Syd a happy birthday. Samantha answered the phone, and Damien started out by thanking her for all she was doing for his dad and saying how much he loved his father.

Then his tone turned confrontational.

"You're not being straight with me, Samantha."

"I beg your pardon," she responded.

"Not sure if you've got the whole story or you're both shittin' me," Damien added.

When she told Damien Syd decided not to follow the recommended new drug treatment plan, Damien started yelling, "Does he know he can die if he does nothing?"

"He's in denial. But you know him—selective hearing," Samantha replied.

"I need to come to Florida and straighten him out," Damien said.

"You should discuss it with your father," Samantha said, then handed the phone to Syd. She was very disturbed by Damien's attitude.

"My son, my son," Syd said enthusiastically as he was handed the receiver.

"Happy birthday, Dad. I'm coming to Florida to see you for myself and talk to your doctors," Damien announced.

Syd put the phone on speaker so Samantha could hear Damien.

"There's no need. Samantha's very involved and can tell you everything," Syd replied.

"I don't believe either of you. I want to hear it from the source," Damien countered.

"If I listened to you three years ago and did chemo, I'd be dead like all the old coots in my building," Syd yelled.

"How can you say that?" Damien yelled back. "By the way, is all of this medical care you're getting covered by insurance?"

"You're out of line," Syd said in a low, serious voice.

"You have no idea how this is distracting me," Damien said. "I have a business to run and your medical problems are preventing me from doing what I need to do."

Samantha felt heartbroken on Syd's behalf. There was no love in this son's voice.

"Blaming me for your failures as usual. Get over it," Syd yelled.

"I should be in charge. That's my job as your son. She's only your girlfriend," Damien insisted.

"Samantha's more than my girlfriend. She's the love of my life," Syd announced.

This statement made Damien furious because it meant that his mother was not the love of Syd's life. Samantha felt a wave of warmth come over her.

"Dad, it's not right," Damien screamed and hung up.

Syd went quiet, put the phone down, and sat on the bed next to Samantha. She felt an overwhelming sadness for him. She couldn't imagine such a conversation with Bobby. Syd had no reaction; he wasn't upset or surprised. He just held her hand.

Samantha, already weary with Syd's medical issues, and now, with Damien taking such a nasty tone, was nearly over the edge. She smelled trouble and weighed her options.

* * * *

Marcel canceled that day's support group and called an emergency meeting in the viewing room to review the recent Samantha and Syd developments. He felt they needed to re-group and decide if intervention was necessary. Personally, he was pleased; either way, Samantha would be free to be with him and it could happen sooner than expected. He often thought about his last encounter as Max, the French hair stylist and having physical contact with her as he styled her hair. There was such electricity between them. Carmella arrived in the viewing room first, looking like she did in the old days with teased blonde hair, loud-colored clothes, and chunky heels. Marcel looked at her with raised eyebrows.

"I liked the old me. I told the council, 'take or leave it, fellas'. If they don't like it, they can shove it."

"Playing with fire," Marcel warned her.

Jake and Mimi arrived, looking concerned. They were fully aware of the new turn of events that could jeopardize the Syd and Samantha relationship.

Once they were all seated comfortably, Marcel grabbed the

remote and flashed a montage of Syd and Samantha photos in various locations.

"Look, they sparkle together. He clearly adores her and she is deeply attached to him. Youse guys oughta be happy," Carmella said, directing her comments to Jake and Mimi.

Marcel freeze-framed an image of a much thinner Syd and Samantha in bed half-naked.

"Do you have to, Marcel?" Jake asked.

"The way Syd's going, he won't be able to do that much longer." Mimi giggled, pointing to the image of them in bed.

"Amazing! That fucker is on the way out and he can still get it up!" Jake remarked.

"So what's the problem, already?" Mimi asked.

"Do you realize Samantha's ready to bolt?" Jake asked Mimi loudly.

Mimi's mood changed; she nodded and became emotional. "I know and it's killing me."

They all gave her the "but-you're-already-dead" look.

Jake piped up, "That would ruin your grand plan of Syd dying in love. You think your darling son is going to be caring and loving? He's a fucking monster."

"Yeah, what's up with that?" Carmella asked Marcel. "I guess you didn't count on that whack-job getting in the way."

Mimi was more upset with Carmella than Jake. Calling Damien a whack job seemed worse than calling him a monster. "How dare you?" Mimi jumped up and yelled in Carmella's face.

"I call it like it is, missy," Carmella responded, putting her hands up to defend herself.

Mimi felt responsible for bringing Damien onto the Earth. She knew she gave birth to a tortured soul who could bring no joy to anyone until he ascended to the spirit world and underwent transformation. She couldn't allow him to ruin Syd's Earth life.

"They are all on a journey," Marcel responded. "We need to respect that."

"Marcel, this whack...I mean, this guy threatens to derail them," Carmella said.

"There's still a chance that Jake can fulfill his wish and speak through Syd. This may pull Samantha back in but it's not a given," Marcel warned.

"Then let's do an intervention. Get Damien of their fucking way," Carmella proposed.

"What if it's not successful?" Mimi asked.

Carmella added, "Foolproof plan. I'll go down as Camille—that hot little number from the salon—and distract Damien; get him to back off Syd and Samantha."

Marcel frowned but Carmella ran out of the viewing room before Marcel could stop her.

"Let's see what's she's up to. Hope that ditz doesn't make it worse," said Marcel as he grabbed the remote and flashed an image of Damien at a bar drinking shots while Camille, the makeover lady, slithered up to him and whispered in his ear.

"I can't hear what she's saying. Turn that volume up," insisted Mimi as she stood up and leaned closer to the image.

"A promise of pussy and free coke and not cola." Marcel responded. *"Oy vey!"* Mimi exclaimed and collapsed on the sofa.

"Don't think of drugs and sex will keep Damien at bay for very long unless Carmella arranges for him to OD, which was definitely not part of the plan." Marcel remarked.

"Shame on you," said Mimi.

Jake move to a corner seat, rested his head in his hands, and closed his eyes.

Marcel walked over, put his arm on his shoulder and said, "I can see your love for Samantha is still overwhelming as you watch her struggle with Syd."

"She's reliving my illness all over. This was all about me and for me. I feel guiltier now than I did before," Jake replied tearfully.

Marcel was pleased Jake had the epiphany but needed somehow to help him work it to his advantage.

"How do we undo this?" Jake asked Marcel.

"It's too late; they're too attached, too connected. Remember, they're soul mates and you have already insinuated yourself into the situation," Marcel said.

"What?" Jake asked.

"Syd is already tuning in to your feelings. Train left the station. Can't stop it now," Marcel responded.

Marcel felt guilty as well. At least he had a game plan to make it up to Samantha. He would sweep down and become her guardian and lover on Earth. The Heavenly Council had practically agreed to it.

"Okay, I get it; but can we make sure we make it right afterwards?" Jake asked.

"She will have to fulfill the mission, heartbreaking though it may be. Syd's listening to Samantha. He wants to prolong his life now and bask in her love."

Marcel stopped talking when he heard the sound of Carmella's chunky heels outside the viewing room.

Carmella entered as suddenly as she left.

"Mimi, you owe me, hon," Carmella announced as she walked in holding a document which she handed to Marcel.

"For offering my son sex and drugs?" Mimi asked.

Carmella sat down on an overstuffed chair. "I bought you time, boys. I got her son away from Syd and Samantha, at least temporarily."

"Where did you get this document?" asked Marcel.

"It was pinned to the doorframe. Looks important," Carmella said.

"I am being summoned before the council. Shit!" Marcel said standing up and looking outside the portico to see who delivered it.

"I didn't hear or see anyone. These Council people have too much power. They need a little socialism up here. Can we go back to the Damien problem? " Jake asked

'I can't deal with this now." Marcel said. He had more important matters to attend to, including the summons to appear before the Heavenly Council. He was concerned that he would be reprimanded for returning to Earth again as the French hairdresser and allowing Carmella's intervention. He wasn't prepared for the real reason he was called.

* * * *

He donned the white robe and entered the chamber. Only Madame was present. She seemed calmer and less formal than on the previous occasion. She asked him to come closer to the dais she could speak to him without the microphone. She made small talk and asked how Carmella was doing as the new support-group leader. Marcel was puzzled until she cleared her throat, adjusted her tiara, and said she had important news for him.

"You are being recommended for a place on the Heavenly Council," Madame announced.

Marcel perked up.

"Not just any place...but my right-hand assistant and my possible successor," she added.

Marcel knew there hadn't been a male Council head for many millennia. This was the opportunity of a thousand lifetimes. He couldn't believe it. He was being invited to a position of immense power. There were so many perks and advantages to the cushy job: access to all the great spirits and guides and luxury housing. Maybe he could entice God to come back as a consultant. What would he have to give up, an Earth life?

Madame knew what he was thinking and confirmed his suspicions by saying, "You realize that you cannot return to Earth ever again if you accept this position."

That was it; it was either join the Heavenly Council or return to Earth. If he did go down to Earth to be with Samantha, when he returned to the spirit world, there was no guarantee as to what level he would be at. He might have to start his spiritual journey all over again.

Madame gave him final instructions that he was not to meddle any longer with the Syd and Samantha match. It had a life of its own. She explained it in a very calm and loving way.

"Marcel, understand that Earth souls have free will. You can give them direction, suggestions, and encouragement, but they will take matters into their own hands." She explained that Syd and Samantha would need to accept and deal with the outcome. Marcel could choose to return to Earth and help Samantha pick up the pieces. If he joined the council, he could ensure that Samantha would be taken care of in the spirit world. However, he couldn't have both.

She told him she needed his decision very soon.

* * * *

Marcel returned to the viewing room, where Jake and Mimi were watching Samantha groom a very weak Syd. She was gently giving him a shave. Then she clipped the hairs around his ears and nose. He took her hand and kissed it. He had tears in his eyes.

Jake and Mimi were unusually quiet and were emotional as they watched.

"I knew this day would come, but watching it is very difficult," Mimi said. "I feel so bad for Samantha. Syd's a shadow of his former self. He looks nothing like he did when we married."

"I'm to blame," Jake said. "If I hadn't gotten that horrible disease, controlled myself, this would never have happened."

Marcel sat in front of both of them.

"I'm glad you two are finding common ground. It shows development."

"Common ground?" Jake said. "The only common ground we have is we're both dead and our spouses are deeply in love."

Mimi wept. "It's over, Jake. Syd's dying and Samantha will move on, or maybe she'll end up here soon from the disease you gave her."

"Shut the fuck up," Jake said. He raised his hand to strike her when Marcel intervened.

Chapter Eighteen

The Break-Up

The blood infusion had only a temporarily positive effect on Syd's stamina. He rallied for a week, during which he danced and screwed with the vitality of a twenty-year-old. Then Samantha noticed he slept a lot and all his appetites were diminishing. Samantha imagined that each time they had sex could be the last.

He still managed to sell some doors and windows. He could still drive the Jag in the crazy Florida traffic and get himself to the pool daily for exercise.

Then Samantha noticed his handwriting became shaky and his A-to-Z lists were harder to read. Syd said he believed he could get his appetite and strength back. Samantha bought him more vitamin supplements and organic foods. She proposed he try a macro-biotic diet. When she described what it meant, Syd looked disgusted.

"Whatever you do, you need to believe in it." Samantha said adamantly.

Syd nodded his head.

"Even if you want to eat shit, believe that it will cure you," she added.

Samantha maintained that years of bad eating contributed to his bad health. She often told him, "Had I been around, you wouldn't have had a heart attack on my watch."

* * * *

Mimi took offense at this. "What nerve. She blames me for his bad health?"

"Cool your jets, Mimi. You were with Syd how many years? Five, seven? He's lived for more decades without you, eating crap," Jake noted.

"We only ate at the best restaurants," Mimi responded.

"You never cooked, did you?" Jake asked.

"Occasionally a roast," Mimi said, pursing her lips.

"Samantha's a fabulous cook and Syd knows that. She's spot-on when she says had she been around, he wouldn't be in the shape he's in," said Jake.

Mimi smirked.

* * * *

Samantha would've intervened earlier with Syd's prostate cancer, cajoled him into less invasive treatments, and taken an active role in his recovery. It was clear to her that it was very late in the game for any miracle cures, and his stubbornness was not helping. With every new pain he developed, her heart broke a little more. She worried about his finances. Would he have enough to live comfortably?

Something is wrong with this picture, Samantha thought, as her own father, ten years older than Syd, was in better physical condition than her boyfriend. But then, Syd could go on for years and fade away slowly.

Both Samantha and Syd observed elderly residents in her condo development in Florida who were wheelchair-bound and looked half-dead. A man of Syd's former vitality and ego would want a certain quality of life. Samantha secretly wished Syd wouldn't suffer and the end would be swift but she would give all her energy to his well-being.

"Doing nothing is not working," she said to him one morning, as she walked him over to the bathroom scale. "You've lost twenty pounds since we met."

"I figured as much. I've tightened my belt several notches," he remarked.

Syd swam in his clothes, especially his suits. Samantha bought him slim jeans and tight-fitting shirts. For a while, he looked quite sexy, fit, and tanned. You would never know he had advanced cancer.

Syd dreaded the idea that Samantha was about to take an extended trip to Asia. She halfheartedly tried to get out of the Asia trip but was secretly looking forward to a temporary break from Syd's aches and pains. He always supported her professional commitments and wanted her to excel at her job and not anger the management.

"I don't want you to jeopardize your job. I'll be fine," Syd said.

Damien surfaced by phone from Vegas after falling off the radar for two weeks. She reluctantly suggested that he visit Syd while she was away in Asia, but he said he was too busy with a big real estate deal. Syd didn't want him around in any case.

Concerned that Syd would stop eating entirely, she hired a lively Dominican woman, to come daily and prepare his lunch while she was away. At first, Syd was skeptical, and asked if Ramona was "colored."

"Half—a mulata." Samantha assured him.

Ramona was high-spirited and made him laugh, so he agreed.

"Meester Seed, okay, dun't worry," Ramona would say, rolling her *r*'s.

Ramona also believed in white magic and placed unidentifiable objects in the freezer.

"What's this?" Syd asked her while holding up a frozen doll made out of yarn.

"Make you esstrong, Meester Seed," Ramona replied.

Syd made veiled racist comments about Ramona and voodoo. Samantha dismissed the doll in the freezer as an oversight, not wanting to spook him. Samantha let Ramona try to expel evil spirits. Syd's inaction wasn't curing him so maybe a frozen doll would.

* * * *

While Samantha was away, Syd had a lot of free time alone to contemplate the future or how much he had left. He felt guilty about all the time and energy Samantha spent taking care of him. He decided to test her and questioned Samantha's commitment to be with him long-term on their daily phone chats.

"Why do you want to be with poor old, sick Syd?" he asked. "You need to go out and find a younger, richer man."

"Do you think that's so easy? Go to the bar on the corner and find some guy just like that?" Samantha quickly replied.

"You need a man to meet your physical needs. I can't anymore," Syd insisted.

She was upset that he challenged her devotion and dismissed their attachment.

"I don't want to hold you back. It's not fair to you," Syd continued.

"We shouldn't be having this discussion on the phone," Samantha said, blowing her nose. Then she asked, "Don't you want to fight for me, for us?"

"Syd's dying," he said.

Samantha hated when Syd talked about himself in the third person. He didn't do it often but she found it annoying and egotistic. She was confused because the day before, he spoke about the latest window deal and going to a trade show in Miami.

Samantha was stressed by a traffic-snarled, polluted Shanghai and local-office Chinese politics. Now, dealing with Syd long-distance made her quite fragile.

"If that's what you want, you need to release me. I'm not going on my own steam. I love you with all my being," Samantha said, sobbing.

"I would never release you. I love you deeply and totally," Syd replied. "I just needed to hear those words."

After her trip to Asia, they agreed to meet back in New York to celebrate their one-year anniversary and to find a new apartment together as the Colony apartment sale was about to close. They needed to move out.

Syd backed out and wanted to stay in Florida.

"I need the sun," he said.

Samantha was furious, as she was being left to pack and move all their belongings.

"Why is it up to me to find us a place to live?" she asked him.

"I just don't want to travel." Syd said, ignoring her question and refusing to return to New York.

She was unaware of just how sick he was and took this as rejection. It was her opportunity to retreat from a difficult situation. She was ready to leave Syd to fend for himself, find his own place to live, and wallow in the dysfunction of his family.

Samantha didn't want to make a decision on the phone but felt compelled. In a wave of anger, she announced, "I'm moving into my own place."

"Is that your final decision?" Syd asked solemnly.

"Yes, it is—with deep regrets," she responded.

* * * *

Judy rushed over after talking to Syd. She heard there was trouble. Samantha dreaded telling Judy that she was leaving.

"I'm going to leave. Can't take it," Samantha said tearfully. She thought Judy would try to convince her to stay, but it was the opposite.

"I'm talking to you like a mother now," Judy advised. "He doesn't deserve you. You're too good for him. Why do you need the aggravation already?"

Judy was angry.. She grabbed her mobile and called Syd. Samantha was impressed. Judy lashed out in a tirade about how stupid he was for not trying to save his relationship with Samantha.

"You're *meshuga*. She's the best thing that ever happened to you. The most devoted woman you could ever find. If you lose her, you're an idiot," Judy screamed, but Syd remained silent.

* * * *

Jake and Mimi interrupted Marcel and Carmella during a support-group meeting. There was a crisis brewing.

"Samantha's throwing in the towel. It's over. Syd's about to die alone," Jake announced.

"Intervention is needed," Marcel said.

"What can we do?" asked Jake.

"You will need to speak through Syd," responded Marcel.

Jake was conflicted. Part of him was glad Samantha was about to dump Syd. Serves him right, he thought. But then he thought about the benefits of her following through and the spiritual brownie points.

"You promised me I could tell Sam how much I love her. Syd needs to do this face to face. Looks like he isn't going anywhere." Jake said.

Marcel realized Jake was not going to play ball he appealed to Carmela. "I'll do one better. Let me swoop down there, distract that lousy ingrate drug addict and give Sam a little morale support to stick it out," Carmella proposed. Mimi felt helpless, consumed with a mix of jealousy and fear that Syd would die alone. She knew Syd would get seriously ill at some point but was not prepared for his rapid deterioration. She had to detach and hope Samantha would stay.

Marcel knew Samantha's compassion and devotion would

come through. Just let Damien send them over the edge; then they would reconcile.

"Trust me. Damien's monstrous attitude will send them back into each other's arms," Marcel said.

Jake and Mimi were skeptical.

Just before Marcel left the gazebo, he threw a wrench into their plans.

"I'm going to do what I can. I hate to bring this up, but we may need to deal with interference from the newly dead Argentine, Alfonso," Marcel said with a groan and headed for the doorway. As he exited the gazebo, he said, "If he comes by, tell him GPYF is not taking any new members or send him to that new committee setting up Facebook and Twitter accounts."

"Facebook and Twitter for the dead?" asked Jake.

"Another way of connecting with earthly loved ones. Hey, Alfonso was probably RC. Send him on a wild-goose chase to find God."

"RC?" Jake asked.

"Roman Catholic," Marcel responded.

"You deal with him. He's your fucking problem," Mimi screamed at Jake.

"My fault?" Jake asked.

Mimi pointed at Jake. "The dead bipolar Latin lover is your problem. He was your match for Samantha before Syd."

"I should have waited to go back to Earth myself and not matched Samantha with anybody," Jake said.

"Why don't you just give in," Mimi said to Jake. "There's nothing we can do except hope for the best. If Samantha bolts, she bolts. Honestly, if I were in her shoes, I wouldn't stick around."

"You bitch; you admit it? This was a bad deal for Samantha," Jake said.

"I wouldn't say a bad deal, but maybe not the best one. I kind of feel sorry for her. She'll have to start over again," Mimi said.

"You owe her now," Jake said.

"Let's not go that far," Mimi responded.

"We'll let the council decide," Jake warned.

"Big man, you think the council is going to do something to me? I'm already in purgatory, wearing this friggin' dress since I died. I spend all my time up here trying to make things right for Syd, and now he's about to check out from down there and check in here. I'm done," Mimi said.

* * * *

Samantha packed boxes and suitcases. She found a new place to live in her old neighborhood in the village. She looked forward to a fresh start and did an A-to-Z list of the benefits of living alone.

Syd called and, in a monotone voice, said he would return to New York in a few days. Judy's boyfriend would pick him up at the airport.

Samantha was horrified when Syd shuffled into the apartment, emaciated and weak. He looked like he had just walked out of Auschwitz. He suffered from severe back pain. His mouth and tongue were numb from a growth in his jaw he could feel from the inside

The Jag was being shipped from Florida, and he had packed up all his stuff and moved out of Samantha's condo.

He headed straight to the bedroom and sat on the bed, still in his overcoat. He said, "No need to fear I'll jump you. As you can see, I'm too weak."

They spent the next several days and nights barely speaking to each other. They lie in the king-sized bed side by side without touching.

Samantha continued cooking for him and packing her stuff. She noticed Syd no longer made the A-to-Z lists and didn't read the newspaper. Normally he would devour every page and highlight the articles for her in red.

He said he made an arrangement with the new owners to rent the co-op month-to-month for four thousand a month. He said he had no energy to move, but she shouldn't worry about him, as he had so many friends in the building he could rely on.

Samantha doubted any of these superficial relationships with mostly elderly people would be of any help. Who could help him navigate his obviously grave health? Judy had told Syd not to count on her; she had her own problems.

"Don't count on me, *bubbelah*. Arnold is severely constipated and I know that's why he can't get it up," Judy said.

Samantha thought, *Syd's dying of cancer and Judy's worried about Arnold not taking a shit.*

Despite the fact Samantha was packed and ready to move out, she orchestrated Syd's medical appointments. He realized he couldn't manage on his own and allowed her to take over. She arranged his doctor visits, paperwork, lab tests, and helped him pay his bills.

Samantha called his doctor and reported how much pain he was in. But the receptionist said he couldn't see him for two weeks. Syd was obviously not a popular patient. He had antagonized the doctors so much, no one from his medical team would see him on an urgent basis. Only his old friend, Doctor Saul Meyer, would see him. He preferred this to going to an emergency room, probably because he knew Meyer would tell want he wanted to hear.

According to Syd, Saul said, "If you need painkillers; I can give you a prescription. Go and enjoy your life."

"What the hell kind of a doctor is this?" Samantha screamed.

"That's what the man said," Syd said nonchalantly.

Samantha blurted out, "You can barely walk; you've lost fifty pounds. You have a growth in your jaw and the guy wants to give you pain pills?"

* * * *

Samantha consulted with Judy daily now. Samantha asked if she should move or stay and added, "Judy, he has nobody."

"You're right; he has no one. I'm no good. Some days I can't get out of bed," Judy said.

"He thinks all his friends in the building are going to come to his rescue."

"Sure, they're good for a casserole here and there. But if someone needs to come and wipe his ass? Forget about it," Judy responded.

When Damien got wind of the news that Samantha and Syd were breaking up, he saw an opportunity to take control. As usual, Syd would put Damien on speakerphone. He called Syd daily to push him to change his documents. Samantha should no longer be in charge. He said Alana and Fiona offered to move in and become caregivers. Then he warned, "Dad, you need to move out of The Colony and into a cheaper apartment. Four thousand a month will wipe you out."

Samantha was horrified. What business was it of his how Syd spent his money? Damien also yelled at Syd for going to an oral surgeon for his numb jaw, as he claimed it was not covered by insurance.

She sat at the foot of the bed, looking at Syd, and a wave of emotion enveloped her. In a flood of tears, she said, "I can't believe your own son would say those things. It makes me very angry and so sad for you. You don't deserve this."

Syd remained silent and tried hard to compartmentalize Damien's heartless words.

Then Samantha asked, "Do you want Alana and her girl-friend to move in and take care of you?"

Syd waved his hands in a gesture that said, 'absolutely not'. "Forget about it. Not happening."

Samantha's mind was racing, but she was committed to seeing him through to the end—whether it was months or years. She would find a way if his money ran out. He could move in with her.

Samantha composed herself and said, "If you want, I'll stay and protect you, make you comfortable, and get you the care you need."

Syd looked into her eyes with longing. The mood shifted as they stared intensely into each other's eyes. At that moment, they instantly forged a united front and a love bond on a new level.

* * * *

Jake pushed through his guilt and sadness, continuing to send energy down to Syd to radiate his love for Samantha. Mimi was simultaneously relieved and jealous at the deeper connection they were witnessing between Samantha and Syd. They had to admit that Marcel was right not to do another intervention. Damien's latest tirade against Syd and Samantha sent them back into each other's arms.

* * * *

Syd used all his strength to extend his hand and pull Samantha closer. She climbed onto the bed, caressed his face, and gently kissed his lips.

"I wish I could feel your luscious lips against mine, but my mouth is all numb," he said.

She lay down beside him and they held hands in silence.

Chapter Nineteen

Transitions

When Syd stopped making his A-to-Z lists, and didn't insist on the daily Love Meter or reading the *New York Times*, Samantha knew he was on a downward spiral. The speed of his deterioration mirrored the rapid pace of their whirlwind romance. Syd's energies were dwindling, the pain increasing, and his quality of life diminishing.

Some days, he accepted that he was near the end; and on others, he wanted to stay alive. He realized he needed to let Samantha take over his life. He felt very lucky that she decided to remain by his side. He didn't want to imagine what would've happened if they had broken up and she moved out. Who else would've taken care of him?

Samantha usually showed courage and strength when it came to Syd's care. At other times, she would get caught up in waves of emotion, especially when she had *déjà vu* from Jake's illness.

When Syd said, "After I'm gone, you'll have a happy life," it sent shivers down Samantha's spine. Jake had said the exact same thing a week before he died.

Samantha knew "happy life" was bullshit. She had a very long grieving process when Jake died and there was no such thing as "happy" for many months. She was also surprised that Syd forgot about grieving over Mimi's sudden death.

Syd told Samantha as he lay in bed, "Always stay young and beautiful." He warned her to avoid any weight gain. Even in his weakened state, he was obsessed with physical appearance.

Then Syd mentioned a new man just as Jake had on his death bed. Syd put a time frame on it. He predicted, "You'll meet someone new within a year. You deserve someone who'll do everything for you."

Samantha responded flippantly, "Fat chance finding a guy who could deal with my HIV status."

Syd dismissed her and said, "You can have any man you want."

It was a statement Samantha didn't believe. Besides, she couldn't fathom another relationship. *Didn't anybody realize how emotionally numb and drained you become, watching someone die?* She also thought about how much more concealer she used now than when Jake was dying.

She *did* notice an enormous difference between the two sick men. While Jake was distant and remote, Syd was the polar opposite. Even in pain and agony, Syd remained emotionally connected, tender, and expressive. He would kiss her hand and tell her how much he loved her several times daily.

"When you're not here—I cry, thinking about how you take care of me," Syd said.

Samantha stayed focused on keeping him comfortable and alleviating his severe pain. She knew that any number of events could send him over the edge. Physically, he was very weak, but his voice was strong and his mind alert as he was not yet on heavy pain meds.

She handled his financial affairs, as he could barely sign his name to checks. However, it was unclear yet how much money he really had. If he ran out of money, she would find a way to care for him. She would move him into her new apartment if needed. She was determined to give him the best quality end-of-life.

Samantha was finally able to get Syd to his original doctor, despite Syd's protests. The new tests showed his bone marrow riddled with metastasized cancer.

The doctor sounded annoyed and frustrated that, in the past, Syd hadn't taken any of his advice. Now there were several end-stage drug treatments that were a long shot, but Syd wasn't interested.

"You're a very sick man," the doctor said. "If anyone told you couldn't die from this, they were *wrong*."

So much for Doctor Saul Meyer's prognosis, Samantha thought.

Syd needed an immediate blood transfusion, kidney function tests, and lung aspiration for fluid. He resisted going into the hospital but Samantha insisted. It was the best place for him to be at that moment. Samantha promised she would get him home as soon as possible. She would take it day by day, but now with a multitude of specialists, tests and treatments.

Syd was placed in a hospital bed next to a semi-comatose elderly Irishman, Mister Mulroney, who was in kidney failure. Syd would make faces when Mister Mulroney would groan, cough, or have an episode. All Syd wanted was to go home, be out of pain, and regain the feeling in his lips and mouth.

"Do something so I can feel my lover's lips," he yelled out.

* * * *

The nurses and doctors found Samantha and Syd a curious couple. Samantha was unashamed to call him her partner and a few were interested in hearing their unconventional love story. As always, Syd remained proud and would complain if Samantha didn't have enough lipstick on when she came to the hospital.

On the first night, the lab techs came to draw blood. Syd held Samantha's hand and said, "I'm imagining you in the nude. It helps me through the pain."

When a nurse took his dinner order, Samantha helped him make his choices. Syd mentioned to the nurse, "This woman thinks food is as important as sex."

Syd went on to tell the nurse about the importance of the Love Meter.

On the first Sunday night with limited hospital staff, Samantha was forced to deal with Syd after they gave him a strong laxative. After helping him to the toilet, she wiped him down repeatedly for an hour.

She thought, *no need to be concerned about a wrinkled ass.* He was so emaciated, he had only skin over bone.

She vowed it was the last time she would deal with his bodily functions. They had to hire help when, and if, they got him home.

Once Samantha got Syd cleaned up, he said, "I have a major complaint. You haven't sung for me in ages."

Singing was the last thing Samantha had on her mind after spending an hour in the bathroom wiping him down. After she got Syd back into bed, she sat by his side, held his hand, and halfheartedly sang *"The Nearness of You."*

Syd smiled contentedly. Mister Mulroney also enjoyed it enough to hum along.

As she was ready to leave, Damien called Syd's cell phone. Syd insisted she talk to him, but Samantha wanted to put it off, as she was exhausted. She was trying to get hours in at work, attend to Syd's affairs, and get to the hospital twice a day. The last thing she needed was Damien barking orders and her patience was wearing thin.

However, Syd handed her the phone.

"I'm too busy to come to New York now; get him into hospice," Damien said.

"We are evaluating all options to get him stabilized," Samantha responded politely and diplomatically.

Damien wanted to talk to Syd, but he shook his head 'no'. Samantha handed him the phone anyway; she wanted Syd to get Damien off her back. Syd put the phone on speaker.

"Dad, you need to get the lawyer and change your documents now. Also, I want to talk to the doctors," Damien demanded.

"Samantha is very capable. The doctors have no time to talk to you," Syd replied.

"She's only your girlfriend, Dad," Damien yelled over the phone.

"She knows what she's doing. If I listened to you and had chemo, I would be dead by now," Syd yelled at the top of his lungs.

A nurse came into the room, saw Syd screaming, and quickly left.

Damien then yelled, "You ungrateful bastard. How dare you say that?" He hung up on Syd.

Syd and Samantha exchanged glances when Damien called back, apologized for calling him a bastard and said, "Let me talk to Samantha."

Syd handed her the phone. Damien's voice was still arrogant.

"You're only his girlfriend; I should be in charge."

"I'm here; you're not. There are decisions to be made every hour. I text you with every new development, details about his condition. What else do you want?"

"I want the truth. How long does he have? How much money is there? What's in his will?"

A nurse came in to check Syd's vitals, and Samantha took the opportunity to continue the conversation in the hospital hallway.

"It could be weeks to a few months. As far as money is concerned, we're using it for his care," Samantha said in a low voice.

"What if it runs out? Then what?" Damien asked.

"We'll decide when we get there," Samantha responded. "Right now, he wants to get out of the hospital, go home, and enjoy the view."

Syd called out for Samantha. She returned to his bedside from the hallway. "You're upsetting your father with your hostile tone. This is no time for harsh words and old agendas. This is a time for love," Samantha said to Damien while looking at Syd.

Syd asked for the phone. He told Damien the conversation was over and hung up. "That was a beautiful thing you said to Damien," he said, and then blew her a kiss.

"It's heartbreaking. You don't deserve this. There's not one ounce of love in his voice and it's very bad phone." Samantha started to cry and watched Syd for a reaction.

"What could I have done differently?" Syd asked.

"You'd think you beat the shit out of him every day of his childhood," Samantha said.

"I gave him the best schools, best doctors, expensive vacations, and a new car at eighteen, which he totaled," Syd said.

"I'm crying on your behalf. Why aren't you upset?" Samantha asked through her tears.

"I'm crying too; but I'm also compartmentalizing," Syd responded.

"It's called denial," Samantha said.

* * * *

Samantha smelled trouble with Damien. She wanted to make sure that Syd was in agreement with her handling everything and that it was all documented legally. She called Jerry and told him about Syd's condition; he sent Samantha copies of all the documents. Samantha was indeed legally in charge and had power of attorney.

Jerry came to the hospital and found Syd completely lucid but very weak. He didn't stay long with Syd and ran into Samantha in the hallway. Samantha had only seen Jerry in photos and was taken aback when she saw how short he was and how he dressed like an aging metrosexual. Jerry said

Damien called him to say Syd was not of sound mind and wanted to change his will and power of attorney.

"Damien was high on something," Jerry said. "He tried to convince me to get Syd to change his documents. I told him Syd is perfectly lucid and knows exactly what he's doing, with the right person looking after his interests. That's you, Samantha."

"I'm doing my best. Dealing with Syd's issues is hard enough, but to have Damien on our case is sending me over the edge," Samantha said, holding back tears.

"What would Syd have done without you?" Jerry asked, giving her a supportive hug. Then he looked up into her eyes and asked solemnly, "How long do they say he has?"

Samantha composed herself. Wiping her tears, she said, "Anywhere from a few weeks to a few months."

Jerry shook his head and then held her hand. "He's so lucky to have you, kid."

Samantha's mind started racing, thinking how she would need Jerry's help, and she said, "As soon as Syd is near the end, I will make sure all his bills are paid—including yours."

Jerry motioned that it wasn't necessary.

"Even if I have to cover the expenses myself, I want Syd to die with dignity," Samantha said, choking up.

"Don't worry, hon," Jerry said, patting her arm.

"I want Damien off my back. Can you do that for me?" Samantha asked quietly.

"Consider it done, doll," responded Jerry, shaking his head. He gave her a hug, turned, and left.

Samantha broke down and propped herself against the wall.

* * * *

Jake shook Marcel's arm and begged, "Do something god-damn it Samantha is going through hell. It's a repeat for her."

"It's soon time for you to speak through Syd, that will help her," responded Marcel.

"I want her to feel me come through, to help her," Jake insisted.

"She will," Marcel assured him and gave Jake a hug as he choked up.

* * * *

After Jerry left, Samantha sat with Syd and watched him sleep. Then she saw a nurse enter the room and address the poor Irishman, who appeared not to have any visitors or family.

"Mister Mulroney, Father Matt is doing rounds. Do you want to see him?"

Syd woke up and smiled. "My love, my desire, you're here."

Samantha whispered, "Pretend you're asleep; there's a priest here. My grandfather would say it would ruin his day when he saw a priest on the street."

Samantha and Syd rarely talked religion. Syd gave up observing Jewish holidays and never spoke about Judaism. In fact, Samantha thought he was the only Jew in America who didn't have a family Holocaust story. Samantha, on the other hand, had a complex family history of three generations of atheists.

Samantha saw a young, handsome priest enter the room and muttered, "Mmm! That would make me go to Sunday mass, hmm."

Then she asked Syd, "Did I ever tell you the story of my grandfather being the bastard son of a corrupt priest in Peru?"

Syd nodded.

Mister Mulroney apparently hadn't anything to say, so Father Matt came over to Samantha and Syd and said, "Sorry to disturb you—"

Before he could say another word, Syd blurted out, "Hello, Father, we have a great story to tell you. Samantha, tell him about your grandfather in Peru."

Samantha thought Syd was trying to be controversial. She resisted but he goaded her. "Come on, tell him," he insisted.

Samantha acquiesced and told the handsome priest the story of her grandfather being raised by Father Mateo in Peru, who was probably his father and not his uncle. Then she went into detail about Father Mateo robbing natives in exchange for services.

Marcel/Father Matt was taken aback. How was it possible he never knew this? Padre Mateo was Samantha's great-grandfather? That was why he felt so connected to Samantha.

Jake watched the scene in the hospital room. He was astounded and furious that Marcel was related to his wife. Now he wanted to protect Samantha from Syd and Marcel.

Father Matt took Samantha's hands. She had a rush of electricity through her body, not unlike an orgasm, but it felt more spiritual. Their eyes locked and Samantha heard nothing of what he said next.

"I'm very sorry your family had that experience."

Then he reached for Syd's hand and, while holding Samantha's, he said, "I feel you two are very special people and lucky to have found each other. God be with you." Then he made the sign of the cross.

Samantha took a deep breath and watched the hot priest leave the room.

Syd became stabilized enough to be sent home in an ambulance.

* * * *

The doormen at The Colony, who were used to seeing Syd stroll proudly into the building, watched him arrive lying flat on a gurney.

Samantha had placed a hospital bed near the window.

Judy, with her many connections, helped her find a newly unemployed Jamaican nurse's aide named Carlene. Samantha hired her on the spot.

Carlene, the short and stocky aide, covered her short Afro with a blonde wig. As she greeted Syd with a wide smile, he immediately announced, "I'm going to call you Smiley; let's go dancing."

Syd didn't seem to mind she was "colored."

Damien called soon after and said he was coming to New York the following day.

Syd asked, "Why is he coming?"

"Then tell him not to come," Samantha said.

"But he's my son," Syd said, still hoping his relationship with Damien would turn around. Samantha knew this meant trouble, and Carlene, a mature, intuitive Jamaican native, knew it as well.

Carlene and Samantha were able to settle Syd in the hospital bed with fresh new linens and lots of pillows. Samantha made up the sofa bed for herself. She gave Carlene their bedroom.

"If I had the energy, I'd slip into bed next to you, to feel the warmth of your body against mine," Syd said before he drifted off to sleep.

* * * *

From the time Damien arrived, he created havoc and conflict with everyone in his path. After greeting Syd, he asked, "How much does she cost?" jerking his head toward Carlene. Then, when Samantha was out of the room, Carlene heard him asking Syd for his wallet.

Damien's karma was so negative that when he took the Jag out for a ride, the new brakes failed. The tow truck Samantha called had an accident on the way. When the second tow truck arrived, they found nothing wrong with the brakes. Samantha didn't want to upset Syd, so she dealt with the tow truck on the street and had the valet store the Jag in the garage.

Upstairs, Carlene witnessed Damien badgering Syd.

"She's a gold digger, Dad," Damien said.

"You don't know what you're talking about," Syd said angrily.

"Treat your father with respect, boy," Carlene yelled.

Syd became furious and, with all his meager strength, sat upright in bed. Carlene was alarmed and tried to settle Syd down.

"I'd marry her tomorrow. Consider her my wife. In fact, we are getting married next week—right here at home," Syd said in a strong voice. Then he wasn't sure if he had dreamed this or not. Had he asked Samantha to marry him?

Carlene was delighted. "A weddin' it's gonna be. I'll make my jerk chicken."

"Where's your checkbook?" Damien asked but Syd didn't respond.

Damien went into the kitchen and found the OxyContin. Carlene watched as Damien shook out pills to give to Syd. Carlene grabbed the vial away from him.

"Too many," she screamed.

"You're fired," Damien yelled.

"Only Samantha can fire me, you cheeky boy," Carlene yelled back.

When Samantha heard what had happened, she wondered why Damien would try to keep Syd drugged up if he wanted him to change his power of attorney or his will. It made no sense.

* * * *

For the next forty-eight hours, Damien proceeded to

bad-mouth Samantha all over town to the neighbors, doctors, nurses, doormen, and anyone who called on Syd's cell phone or landline—people Samantha hadn't met. Damien was desperate to take control.

When Samantha heard through the grapevine what was happening, she asked Judy to intervene because she had known Damien for years. Judy arrived to find Damien talking negatively about Samantha to the hospice nurse and asking what facility he could send Syd to for free. The nurse shook her head and told him there was no such place. Then he told the nurse he would get rid of Carlene. The nurse filled out her documentation and quickly left.

Judy heard Damien, became deeply upset, and yelled, "That's not your decision. You are doing nothing of the kind."

Damien smugly announced, "Alana and Fiona have offered to come and take care of Syd for free. All they want is room and board."

Judy screamed, "Alana? Are you crazy?"

Samantha returned to the apartment in time to hear Judy railing at Damien.

"Alana?" Samantha asked.

"Alana was here with Fiona this morning. They offered to care for him for free."

"One look at those two sloppy dykes will probably send Syd permanently to never-never land," Judy said.

"I know. Syd hates looking at them. Besides, Alana and Fiona are broke. They would clean him out. Where are they going to sleep?"

"In the bedroom," Damien said. "You sleep out here with Dad every night. You don't need the bedroom."

"You're irrational. Get this straight. Carlene stays as long we need her."

"Dad said he was leaving Alana something in his will. By the way, I want to know what's in his will anyway. I asked him earlier and he wouldn't tell me," Damien replied.

Judy became livid. "This is no time to be discussing that. You're heartless! You disrespect this woman, whom your father loves deeply, and who is selflessly taking care of him by making a peaceful and loving environment for his final days. You're destroying it!"

Damien waved her away and returned to Syd's bedside. A flustered Judy clasped her chest and whispered to Samantha,

"I can't take this. I need a Valium."

Judy hugged Samantha and said, "Go, take care of Syd. He needs you, not that bastard of a son."

As Judy left and closed the door, Samantha heard Damien say to Syd, "That Judy's a bitch, Dad."

Samantha couldn't hear Syd's response. She called out to Damien to come into the kitchen.

"Can I ask why you want Syd's checkbook?" Samantha asked him.

"Because I came here with no money," Damien replied.

"I'll give you money; how much do you need?" Samantha asked.

"I don't want your money," Damien snapped back.

"Why did you come then?" Samantha asked.

"I need closure. Forty years of stuff between us to sort out," he responded.

Samantha lost her cool. "This is not about you. This is about your father."

"Also, I need to straighten him out. He's dying; he's not ever going to drive the Jag again or go back to work."

"That's what keeps him going—thinking he's going to get better and jump into the sofa bed with me. Why the fuck would you take that away from him?"

Samantha took a deep breath and a booming voice said to Damien, "You arrived angry and hostile with no rational game plan, only accusations and attempts to sabotage efforts to make Syd comfortable and help him die with dignity."

She stopped before she became emotional, then regained her composure and announced, "We *will* spend all his money doing it. You'll be lucky to be left with the Jag, if you don't total it."

Damien didn't respond. He went over to Syd, who had slept through the tirade, woke him up, and asked if he wanted Chinese takeout. Syd was too groggy to respond. But Damien left to get Chinese food anyway.

Samantha was bombarded by Damien from all sides. She developed heart palpitations and knew she needed to calm down. She decided to go to the office for a few hours the next day. Before she left, she asked Syd, "Are you okay with Damien here?"

Syd responded weakly, "Not sure."

Samantha nuzzled up close to Syd and then spoke in a

quiet voice. "When I get back from the office, we need to talk about Damien. He's creating a very uncomfortable environment here and your Smiley wants to quit." Syd squeezed her hand and raised it to his lips and kissed it.

* * * *

Damien contemplated selling the OxyContin on the street or keeping Syd drugged. The hospice nurse said she would call in the prescription for liquid morphine but would come by and help train Carlene to administer it.

Damien was thrilled, as the morphine would fetch a higher price than OxyContin. If Syd wasn't going to leave him any money, at least he could sell the drugs.

When the pharmacy delivered the morphine, Damien took out the contents of the package. There were several bottles of liquid and some swabs. He read the directions quickly and approached Syd.

Syd was in a lot of pain but shook his head complaining that the drugs made him too groggy. While Carlene rearranged Syd's pillows, she snarled at Damien as he tried to persuade Syd that his love affair with Samantha was an illusion.

"Why would an attractive woman twenty years your junior be in love with you? Answer: money!" Damien said.

"She has her own money, and she's the love of my life. I want to die in love," Syd said.

"We'll see about that," Damien said.

Damien was determined that no wedding would take place. With Samantha out of the way for a few hours, Damien finally had control.

Damien had the swab in one hand and the liquid morphine in the other. Syd put his hand out to say stop while Damien took a swab, dipped it in the morphine and quickly put it against the inside of his father's cheek.

Carlene cried out, and tried to stop him. Damien then said to her in a low voice, "You want some too?" She was petrified and walked away. Carlene turned around just before she reached the bedroom and watched Damien insert the morphine-drenched swab a second time. A few minutes later, Syd's breathing became more shallow and then stopped.

At that moment, Samantha was hailing a taxi to come home and had a pain in the pit of her stomach. She knew something had happened to Syd. As she was heading home in the taxi, Damien called her cell phone and said, "Dad's gone." Samantha called the hospice nurse, who remarked, "That was fast." Samantha then called Carlene, who locked herself in the bathroom so no one would hear and said, "Lordy, Lordy. Dat boy dun kill his daddy."

Samantha was so shocked she didn't respond. Carlene added, "Mister Syd was walkin' around dah house dis morning. He coulda got strongah, poor soul. Dat boy gonna have to ansah to his makah, soonah or latah."

At first, Samantha was horrified, but then thought maybe Damien had done Syd a favor. Was that Damien's decision to make? When Samantha returned, Damien was on the phone in the kitchen, talking about a Vegas real estate deal. It wasn't until later that Samantha and Carlene realized Damien took away all of Syd's medications.

Samantha stood watching Damien talking on the phone as if nothing major had just happened. Carlene approached her, gave Damien a dirty look, and then gave her a hug. Samantha held back the tears.

Samantha pushed past Damien, who didn't acknowledge her, and gingerly walked into the living room. Carlene followed and took her hand. Samantha took several deep breaths as she approached the hospital bed near the picture window. Syd lay there with his head fallen to one side, just like the way he would fall asleep in front of the TV in his favorite chair.

Carlene left her alone with the lifeless Syd. Samantha put her hand on Syd's forehead and then caressed his cheek. She kissed him on the lips. She could almost feel him kissing her back. She put her head on his chest and sobbed.

Samantha tried to stop crying, remembering it wouldn't help him cross over. In a shaky voice, she sang *"Embraceable You"* but couldn't finish.

Damien was still on the phone. He looked over to a grieving Samantha and smirked. Without saying a word, he downed some pills from his pocket, grabbed the keys to Syd's beloved Jaguar, and left the apartment.

Carlene came back to Syd's bedside. She made comforting circles on Samantha's back and said, "Mister Syd loved you, darling. But dat boy gonna have to ansah to dah big man."

"Someday he'll pay for what he did," Samantha said through her tears.

Carlene looked at Samantha, took a deep breath, and said, "Dat boy not gonna make it back to Vegas."

"You think?" asked Samantha.

"I don't think, *I know*," replied Carlene.

* * * *

Jake, Mimi, and Marcel watched the scene in silence.

"Well Mimi, you got what you wanted in a very fucked up way," Jake remarked. "Old Syd died in love."

"I'm still reeling from watching Damien kill his father. *Oy!*" Mimi said, exhausted.

Jake changed the subject and asked Marcel, "What was the purpose of you going to the hospital as a goddamn priest?"

"It didn't help anybody," Mimi said. "It looks to me like there's some connection between you and Samantha."

"I think we're on to you," Jake said, glaring at Marcel. "Hidden agendas."

Marcel rose and paced.

"I swear it didn't start out like that," Marcel said. "You two were at each other's throats over this match. You failed for so long and it was coincidence that Syd and Samantha were destined. I didn't know she existed. I didn't pay attention to my descendants on Earth. I moved on. Do I look like the corrupt Jesuit priest now? I'm rebranded, redeemed!"."

Jake interrupted, "Wait, she's your great-granddaughter... which somehow makes us related. Oh, Christ! I mean, oh, Bob!"

"Please don't call him here. I'm still embarrassed he was once one of us," Mimi said.

Marcel calmed Jake down. "Get hip to the scene—connected down there and up here."

Jake looked skeptical.

"Hey man; honestly, I didn't know it until the hospital. Even I, so spiritually developed, was clueless. I didn't figure it out until Samantha told her story. I'm just as freaked out about it as you are."

"There's something really creepy about this. You want to be matched on Earth with your own great-granddaughter?" Jake asked.

"It's called reincarnation, asshole. It happens all the time. Someday, you may be fucking your mother from another life," Marcel announced.

"Okay guys, cool it. Hate to put the kibosh on your family reunion but what's next?" Mimi asked.

"Syd's on his way up here, right? What kind of agenda will he have?" Jake asked.

Mimi sat upright and said, "Well, I'm guilt-free. I did my part. Syd died in love, although it looks like at the hands of my son."

"We'll see when we get to the Heavenly Council," Marcel responded.

"I am going back down. I'll do whatever it takes," Jake announced.

Mimi approached Jake. "I'll help you however I can."

Jake looked surprised.

"I'm doing it for Samantha, not you. She's the one who got screwed—twice in fact."

"That's kind of you, Mimi. I hope you get out of this black dress, doll." Jake smiled and added, waving his arms, "I see you in a fuchsia V-neck, A-line dress, Chanel-length, and black high-heel pumps."

"Well, that comment lit up my gaydar," Marcel remarked.

"Only a *fegalah* would know such things," Mimi said.

"Wouldn't you want to head back down to Earth to be with a SAM and not Samantha?" Marcel asked, grinning.

"Fuck you, Marcel," Jake responded and added, "It's cool to bi now. You might want to consider it, *Padre*."

* * * *

After the funeral home took Syd's body, Samantha and Carlene removed the sheets from the bed. Judy arrived and hugged Samantha while Carlene burned incense.

"I tried to give him death with dignity," Samantha said in a whimper.

"You went above and beyond, hon," Judy said while wiping away Samantha's tears.

* * * *

Shortly after a medicated Damien totaled the Jag on the West Side highway and was thrown from the car, he lay on the side of the road with traffic whizzing by.

Chapter Twenty

Revelations

Syd, clad in a white robe, was instructed to enter a glass elevator. After he entered, the doors closed and he ascended on autopilot. When the doors opened, he stepped into a stark white room where a costume cocktail party was in full swing. There was an array of people dressed in clothing from different eras, chatting and drinking from plastic cups. Syd didn't recognize anyone at first.

Jake approached Syd, shook his hand, and introduced himself in a warm, friendly manner. "Jake Becker. We've been communicating, you might say."

"You look and sound familiar," Syd responded. Then he realized who Jake was and blurted out, "Samantha was fabulous when I lost all my bodily functions. I'm sure you already know that."

Jake led Syd to the bar and ordered drinks for both of them. "This is your 'welcome to the other side' party, but we have to talk."

Syd looked at the bare walls and the odd people. He said, "I threw better parties at The Colony."

"Get used to it. It's not what you thought it would be," Jake said.

"That was quite a transition, though. White light, then gorgeous colors; the beauty, the peace, the love, and all the dead relatives, smiling with open arms. Then I end up in this place," Syd said, bemused. He stared into his plastic glass and wondered what the colorless liquid was.

"All that white light, the colors, beauty, and love are a big come-on. Hate to tell you, bud, it's all downhill from here," Jake said.

"You mean I should have read the fine print?" Syd asked, laughing.

"That's why everyone here wants to get back down. If they made us too comfortable, no one would return to Earth," Jake said before downing his drink.

Marcel bounced over to Syd and Jake with a drink in his hand. He pounded Syd on the back and said, "Welcome, Syd. We've been waiting for you."

Mimi joined them. She smiled meekly at Syd and said, "Been awhile."

Syd looked Mimi up and down. "I have nothing to say to you except that you still look fat."

Mimi became livid and lunged towards Syd who stopped her by grabbing her arm.

Marcel noticed Mimi having a meltdown. He wanted to referee but decided to let the discussion take its course; so he had another drink.

Mimi backed down and became apologetic.

"I'm sorry," Mimi said to Syd. "You knew all along that Damien wasn't your son."

"Not until I got here," Syd responded. "You left me with a disturbed kid who took my life prematurely! Why are you here? You should be in hell!"

"Hate to break the bad news, dude, but it's all one place," Jake offered.

Marcel chimed in, "Mimi has been working overtime to make things right."

Mimi raised her voice and said to Syd, "You were dying already. The kid put you out of your misery."

"I would've gotten better and had a few more years with Samantha—the love of my life. But *your* son played God."

Mimi held back what she wanted to say, which was, "Fuck you," but instead said, "You should be thanking us. If it wasn't for us, you would've died alone like a dog. For your edification, we arranged your falling in love with Samantha.

Syd looked around the room. "I feel Samantha crying herself to sleep right now. When can I go back and be with her?" he asked.

"I know how you feel. I think *I* should go back; I've put in my dues," Jake said.

Marcel—a little tipsy—put his arms around Syd and Jake, and said quietly, "I have watched you both fuck up and leave her in tatters. She deserves better. Maybe it's my time to go down and change that."

"Another one playing God...or whoever is in charge here. Somehow, I don't think you clowns have any authority." Syd sneered, removing Marcel's hand from his shoulder.

"Samantha must be some piece of ass," said Mimi as she walked away.

"So you're taking that council job after all?" Jake asked.

"Haven't made up my mind," Marcel said while scanning the room.

Carmella bounced into the room and approached them.

Syd looked puzzled and asked, "Who the hell are you?"

"It's a long story, hon. We'll have cawfee and tawk," Carmella responded.

Marcel chimed in, "I wouldn't make any coffee dates. I heard the council has plans for you, Seaside Psychic."

"Would you believe it? I'm going *back*! The council said I have more value down there, communicating with youse guys up here and giving comfort to Earth souls."

"Do you know who you're going down as?" Marcel asked.

"Remember the make-up artist, Camille?" Carmella responded. "

Marcel then remarked, "A psychic makeup artist."

Syd said, "Max, Camille. Hair, makeup. That was you two? *Oy!*"

With hands on her hips, Carmella announced, "I don't think what you three are up to is right. I'll see to it that you're all busted."

She rushed towards the glass elevator, which opened automatically. As the door closed, she shouted, "Going back down to get my roots and nails done! Hallelujah!"

* * * *

Samantha felt rough for weeks after Syd's death. She wasn't sure if she was shaken up more by his death or by Damien's shenanigans. Carlene was almost right when she said Damien wouldn't make it back to Las Vegas. After totaling the Jag, he was actually dead for a few minutes in the ambulance on the way to the hospital. They revived him but he was in an induced coma.

All she wanted was to get far away from the horror of Syd's final weeks and concentrate on the memory of his love and devotion. She still felt his arms around her at night in bed and his voice calling out to her, "My love, my desire." No one—not the evil Damien—could take that away from her.

Judy became more of a support to Samantha after Syd's death than before. She called Samantha daily and tried to cheer her up. Arnold took Judy and Samantha out for dinners. They helped her pack the rest of her things and move into her new apartment. One day, Judy suggested they have their hair and makeup done at Chez Max. Samantha was reluctant as she was afraid it would remind her of Syd when he was strong and healthy. Judy insisted and off they went to upper Madison Avenue.

As they entered the salon, Chez Max, Samantha felt a twinge of nostalgia but was taken aback by Max. He seemed like an entirely different person, lacking the warmth and energy of her last visit. Max cut Samantha's hair in silence. Judy later remarked that this was his normal demeanor, and what Samantha saw the first time was a different side of Max. "Grumpy today. He probably needs his colon cleansed," Judy remarked.

The makeup artist overheard them and beckoned them into her room.

"Love your bag, looks designer," Camille said to Samantha. Then she asked, "Did you just lose someone?"

Judy looked shaken but Samantha nodded and said, "Yes, and actually, he bought me this bag."

"He says he loves you and he's making a new list," Camille said.

Judy plopped down in a chair, flabbergasted. "Syd's speaking to you?" she asked incredulously. "I'm getting the chills."

"That's not all, sugar. There's another one with him—a Jacob, a Jay?"

"Jake!" corrected Samantha and then added, "I feel like we had this conversation before."

Samantha suddenly realized Camille reminded her of The Seaside Psychic.

"*Oy*, I'm going to faint already," Judy said, fanning herself with a magazine.

Camille whispered to Samantha, "They've been fucking with you big time up there, along with a dead relative of yours."

"Oh, my God! Who?"

"I see a robe, a church, mountains, some foreign place—Matt, Matthew?"

"Padre Mateo, the corrupt priest, my great-grandfather?"

"He's appeared in your life—twice as your hairdresser, then Lyle the headhunter, and a priest in the hospital. He could come back as..." Camille said.

Samantha blew up and said, "Please don't tell me he was also my gynecologist? The thought of my great-grandfather with his hands up my front, feeling my ovaries is just too creepy!"

Camille tried not to laugh. Samantha held her hands in the air and said, "Get that picture out of my mind!"

Judy piped up, "Are there any spirits around me? I often wondered if Arnold is a reincarnation of my father—who couldn't get it up either, according to my mother."

Camille held her hand to her head. "You were set up with Syd by Jake and some woman. That bad priest orchestrated it."

Samantha became angry. "Set up? Am I a pawn in some sick celestial game? I'm being stalked by a dead relative?"

"They wanted to make it up to you because they love you," Camille said.

Samantha was appalled and said, "Fuck them. Look what they did...loved me and died on me. Jake gave me a deadly disease. Then he tries to make up for it by setting me up with a sick old man and his wacko son? Ha!"

Camille nodded and said, "Don't forget about the other dead guy."

"Who?" Samantha asked.

Camille said, "You know, that Spanish guy?"

"Alfonso, the Argentine? Shit! He's sniffing around too?" Samantha said with alarm in her voice.

"He was, but Jake shooed him away," Camille responded.

"The last three men in my life are dead: Jake, Alfonso, and now Syd. What the hell does this mean?" Samantha asked.

"It means you've got connections, up there," Camille said, raising her eyes to the ceiling.

Samantha stood and held up her hand. "Big fucking deal. Look, I forgive Jake for not admitting to being a closet homo, leaving us broke, and giving me the virus—because he gave me Bobby. I forgive Syd for ignoring his cancer because he adored me and showed it. Alfonso was a maniac but left Bobby money, so he's off the hook."

"They all love you," Camille said to Sam.

"Tell them to butt out. I'll find my own guy when I'm ready," Samantha responded.

Then Samantha looked up at the ceiling and yelled, "Did you hear that, boys?"

Camille smiled and said, "Message sent loud and clear, hon."

Samantha continued, "As for this Marcel—my great-grandfather, the ex-priest or whoever he is this week—stay the hell away from me. I'll smoke you out no matter what the disguise."

Samantha grabbed her coat and handbag. Camille followed her to the main door where a good-looking, middle-aged male client arrived. The man smiled at Samantha and asked, "Don't we know each other?"

Samantha gave him a firm, "No." She was suspicious Marcel might be stalking her again. She turned, gave Camille a look, and then stormed out of the salon. She took the stairs instead of the elevator to the lobby, sailed past the doorman, and emerged on Madison Avenue.

Samantha was determined to keep all three dead guys— Jake, Alfonso, and Syd, plus Marcel, her reincarnated great-grandfather—out of her orbit, and control her own future.

* * * *

Jake, Marcel, Mimi, and Syd headed to a hearing before the Heavenly Council. As they entered the chamber, the council members were already seated. They had no time to prepare Syd. They also didn't expect yet another new council president, who was now a gorgeous black woman.

As they entered the chamber, Marcel remarked, "Obviously great believers in diversity. We went from white to yellow to black."

"I don't think you want her to hear that," Jake said.

"I did hear that. We'll deal with you later," said Madame President in a stern voice from the main podium.

"Sounds like your stock ain't so high anymore," Jake whispered to Marcel. He added, "New management, new rules, my friend."

Syd noticed Madame's nameplate and was horrified. "What? Madame? Is this a whorehouse? Heaven run by coloreds? Is God a *schvartze and* a woman?"

"Relax. She's not God; he's on sabbatical," Jake said to Syd and added, "hopefully she didn't hear that."

Marcel was visibly nervous as clearly something had changed with the council. Then Madame President summoned Mimi to the front.

Syd whispered to Jake, "Time to meet her maker and get her comeuppance."

"Missus Miriam Weis, you have shown spiritual development and growth. You selflessly matched your husband and gave him peace. You rose above your emotions and sent your son back down to Earth to face his demons and learn a lesson."

Syd then yelled, "This woman is an adulterer and a liar! What's she talking about? Sending my son back?"

Mimi responded, "Shut up, Syd. Damien totaled your Jag and ended up dead in an ambulance for a few minutes. He was on his way here but I sent him back down. You won't see him up here for a while."

"I'm done with him," Syd said and added, "and with you too."

"If it makes you feel any better, Damien's paralyzed from the neck down," Mimi said.

"He totaled my Jag," Syd exclaimed ignoring the part of Damien being paralyzed.

Madame hit the gavel again for silence.

"As you know, Carmella Santini is on a new Earth assignment so I am appointing Mimi Weis as the new GPYF support-group leader," Madame proclaimed.

Madame President stood and waved her glass gavel. Instantly Mimi shed her black housedress. She was now clad in a fuchsia, Chanel-length, A-line cocktail dress and black pumps.

"It's in my color palette," Mimi remarked, showing off her dress. She turned to Jake. "It's exactly what you recommended!"

"Jacob Becker, please step forward," Madame said.

"Madame President, may I speak?" Jake asked meekly.

"Not really, but give it a try," she responded.

"I ask that I return to Earth and help my wife recover from her latest loss. I want to make up for the wrongs I have done her twice—once on Earth and again here by matching her with him," Jake said, pointing to Syd.

"That was no mistake, buddy. We were and *are* soul mates," Syd declared.

Madame President brought her gavel down twice and said, "Quiet please! Jacob Becker, you will remain here and lead a new initiative to help AIDS victims—now that they are in the millions."

Mimi whispered to Marcel, "See, they know he's a big *fegalah*."

"But...but—" Jake started to say and was interrupted by Madame President.

"I'm not finished. In exchange for your expected contribution, Samantha will no longer have the HIV virus."

Jake thought for a moment. If that was the trade-off, he was happy. He wouldn't get to be with Samantha but at least she would be virus-free.

Marcel was thrilled. Jake was no longer his competition. He wondered what the black leader had in store for him. Then she turned her attention to Syd.

"Sydney Weis, you are owed a better Earth life, as you exited earlier than expected."

Syd scowled at Mimi, who was still admiring her new outfit.

"You can go back to Earth when you wish," said Madame.

"Some get all the breaks," said Jake, looking at Syd.

"Saved me the trouble of presenting my A-to-Z list of why I should go back," Syd said proudly, as he felt he was getting special treatment.

Marcel was appalled and piped up, "Madame President, he hasn't been debriefed, attended spiritual development classes, or support groups."

He realized if he got back to Earth, he would be in competition with Syd. He would take his chances. Marcel decided at that moment to turn down the council position. He could feel Samantha in his arms already.

"Madame, I respectfully decline the offer of a council position. I wish to return to Earth and pursue my soul mate."

Syd got angry. "Who the hell are you?"

Mimi whispered, "If you want to know the truth, Samantha's great-grandfather."

Syd yelled, "You've got to be kidding. That must be illegal."

Madame struck with the gavel again, ordering silence.

"Marcel, you will have an Earth assignment instead of a council position. Unlucky for you, in my last lifetime, I was the product of a corrupt priest who raped my mother so you will go back to Earth as a priest. *A good priest.*"

Marcel, Mimi, and Jake gasped, while Syd smiled.

"You will tend to little children instead of fathering them. Maybe in your next lifetime the church will allow you to marry but don't count on it."

Marcel nodded. He put a positive spin on his assignment, saying to Jake and Mimi, "At least I'm outta here for a while. A chance to recharge, regroup."

Syd thought Marcel sounded like a burned-out corporate executive. It certainly challenged his opinion of Heaven.

Madame had parting words for Marcel.

"Perhaps when we see you again, you will be council material. It's up to you. Don't fuck up."

"Try my best," said Marcel, who immediately was transformed into a 21st Century version of the handsome Padre Mateo and headed to the glass elevator. As the door opened a voice similar to the one that greeted at his death, "Now, go and be a good priest. Last chance, dude."

As the priest gave a thumbs up sign, Syd stopped the doors from closing. He morphed into a middle-aged black man, jumped in the elevator with Marcel, and said, "Game on!"

About the Author:

Angela Page is a writer, film producer, finance professional, and a graduate of The London School of Economics and New York University. She divides her time between Boca Raton and Los Angeles.

Also from Eternal Press:

CARLA CARUSO

Mommy Blogger
by Carla Caruso

eBook ISBN: 9781615727223
Print ISBN: 9781615727230

Romance, Humor
Novel of 68,698 words

One baby, one lie–and a whole new career.

Stella lands a great job as a mommy blogger. The catch is she's never had children. Plunged into a world of insanity every mother faces, she must learn to cope as her lies build upon one another. A sexy ex comes into the picture, forcing her to choose between him or the job and a handsome 'keeper' of a coworker. It can't last forever.

Also from Eternal Press:

Bittersweet

by Laurencia Hoffman
eBook ISBN: 9781629292908
Print ISBN: 9781629292915

Paranormal Romance Fantasy
Short Novel of 48,583 words

Cade and Rowan met when they were young. Their
families have feuded for years but that does not stop
them from developing a friendship that leads to
something more. When Rowan's father learns that they
are seeing one another, a fight breaks out between the
two families. Cade's family is forced to flee for their
lives.

Twenty-five years later, Rowan and Cade meet again by
chance. Their feelings for each other never really left,
but Rowan is now a married woman with a daughter.
They decide to rekindle their romance, even though
they know that danger will follow them.

Visit Eternal Press online at:

Official Website:
http://www.eternalpress.biz

Blog:
http://www.eternalpress.biz/blog/

Reader Chat Group:
http://groups.yahoo.com/group/EternalPressReaders

Twitter:
http://twitter.com/EternalPress

Facebook:
http://www.facebook.com/profile.php?id=1364272754

Google +:
https://plus.google.com/u/0/115524941844122973800

Tumblr:
http://eternalpress-damnationbooks.tumblr.com

Pinterest:
http://www.pinterest.com/EPandDB

Instagram:
http://instagram.com/eternalpress_damnationbooks

Youtube:
http://www.youtube.com/channel/
UC9mxZ4W-WaKHeML_f9-9CpA

Good Reads:
http://www.goodreads.com/profile/EternalPress

Shelfari:
http://www.shelfari.com/eternalpress

Library Thing:
http://www.librarything.com/catalog/EternalPress

Our Ebay Store:
http://www.ebay.com/usr/ep-dbbooks